H E A R T

HEART

Stories of
LEARNING TO LOVE AGAIN

Edited by Kristen Couse
Series Editor, Thomas Dyja

ILLUMINA™

MARLOWE & COMPANY AND
BALLIETT & FITZGERALD INC.
NEW YORK

An Illumina Book™

Published by
Marlowe & Company
A Division of Avalon Publishing Group Incorporated
841 Broadway, 4th Floor
New York, NY 10003

and

Balliett & Fitzgerald Inc.
66 West Broadway, Suite 602
New York, NY 10007

Distributed by Publishers Group West

Book design: Jennifer Daddio

Manufactured in the United States of America

ISBN: 1-56924-642-4

Library of Congress Cataloging-in-Publication Data

Heart: stories of learning to love again / edited by Kristen Couse.
    p. cm. — (Illumina)
    ISBN 1-56924-642-4
        1. Love—Literary collections. I. Couse, Kristen. II. Series.

PN6071.L7H39 2001
808.8'03542—dc21   00-048189

CONTENTS

LETTER FROM THE EDITORS

Many believe that literature cannot change the world, that it should be content to live between its covers, on the shelves, as a decoration to our lives.

But at the most difficult, challenging, complex moments, again and again we reach up to those shelves, finding guidance and solace and drive among the words of great writers. While a novel may not topple a government, it can change hearts, stiffen resolve, light fires, dry tears or cause them to flow and so affect the world along with the millions of other small motions, the seed-carrying breezes and rivulets, that make our planet work.

We have created Illumina Books in hopes of changing your life. Maybe not in earth-shattering ways, but in ways that comfort and inspire, in ways that help you to continue on.

Each Illumina anthology is a careful collection of extraordinary writing related to a very specific yet universal moment; bouncing back from a lost love, for example, or the journey to healing. With the greatest authors as your guides, you'll read the stories of those who have traveled the same road, learn what they did, see how they survived and moved on.

By offering you the focused beauty and wisdom of this literature, we think Illumina Books can have a powerful, even a therapeutic effect. They're meant not just to work on the mind, but in the heart and soul as well.

—*The Editors*

from

ON LOVE

ALAIN DE BOTTON

*It has been said that it is best not to over-analyze love.
Obviously, Alain de Botton doesn't share this belief. In
his first novel, he tracks every phase of the relationship
between his narrator and Chloe, from their chance
meeting on a Paris–London flight, to the moment
when she leaves him, to, in this excerpt, the
process of shedding the incredible weight
that a broken heart can leave behind.*

1. There is an Arabic saying that the soul travels at the pace of a camel. While we are forced ahead by the relentless dynamic of the time-tabled present, our soul, the seat of the heart, trails nostalgically behind, burdened by the weight of memory. If every love affair adds a certain weight to the camel's load, then we can expect the soul to slow according to the significance of love's burden. By the time the animal was finally able to shrug off the crushing weight of her memory, Chloe had nearly killed my camel.

2. With her departure had gone all desire to keep up with the present. I lived nostalgically, that is, with constant reference to my life as it had been with her. My eyes were never really open, they looked backward and inward to memory. I would have wished to spend the rest of my days following the camel, meandering through the dunes of memory, stopping at charming oases to leaf through images of happier days. The present held nothing for me, the past had become the only inhabitable tense. What could the present be next to it but a mocking reminder of the one who was missing? What could the future hold besides yet more wretched absence?

3. When I was able to drown myself in memory, I would sometimes lose sight of the present without Chloe, halluci-

nating that the breakup had never occurred and that we were still together, as though I could have called her up at any time and suggested a film at the Odeon or a walk through the park. I would choose to ignore that Chloe had decided to settle with Will in a small town in Southern California, the mind would slip from factual reporting into a fantasy of the idyllic days of elation, love, and laughter. Then, all of a sudden, something would throw me violently back into the Chloe-less present. The phone would ring, and on my way to pick it up I would notice [as if for the first time, and with all the pain of that initial realization] that the place in the bathroom where Chloe used to leave her hairbrush was now empty. And the absence of that hairbrush would be like a stab in the heart, an unbearable reminder that she had left.

4. The difficulty of forgetting Chloe was compounded by the survival of so much of the external world that we had shared together and in which she was still entwined. Standing in my kitchen, the kettle might suddenly release the memory of Chloe filling it up, a tube of tomato paste on a supermarket shelf might by a form of bizarre association remind me of a similar shopping trip months before. Driving across the Hammersmith flyover late one evening, I would recall driving down the same road on an equally rainy night but with Chloe next to me in the car. The arrangement of pillows on my sofa evoked the way she placed her head down on them when she

was tired, the dictionary on my bookshelf was a reminder of her passion for looking up words she did not know. At certain times of the week when we had traditionally done things together, there was an agonizing parallel between the past and present: Saturday mornings would bring back our gallery expeditions, Friday nights certain clubs, Monday evenings certain television programs . . .

5. The physical world refused to let me forget. Life is crueler than art, for the latter usually assures that physical surroundings reflect characters' mental states. If someone in a Lorca play remarks on how the sky has turned low, dark, and gray, this is no longer an innocent meteorological observation but a symbol of psychological states. Life gives us no such handy markers—a storm comes, and far from this being a harbinger of death and collapse, during its course a person discovers love and truth, beauty and happiness, the rain lashing at the windows all the while. Similarly, in the course of a beautiful warm summer day, a car momentarily loses control on a winding road and crashes into a tree fatally injuring its passengers.

6. But the external world did not follow my inner moods. The buildings that had provided the backdrop to my love story and that I had animated with feelings derived from it now stubbornly refused to change their appearance so as to

reflect my inner state. The same trees lined the approach to Buckingham Palace, the same stuccoed houses fronted the residential streets, the same Serpentine flowed through Hyde Park, the same sky was lined with the same porcelain blue, the same cars drove through the same streets, the same shops sold much the same goods to much the same people.

7. Such a refusal of change was a reminder that the world did not reflect my soul, but was an independent entity that would spin on regardless of whether I was in love or out of it, happy or unhappy, alive or dead. The world could not be expected to change its expressions according to my moods, nor the great blocks of stones that formed the streets of the city to give a damn about my love story. Though they had been happy to accommodate my happiness, they had better things to do than to come crashing down now that Chloe was gone.

8. Then, inevitably, I began to forget. A few months after breaking up with her, I found myself in the area of London in which she had lived and noticed that the thought of her had lost much of the agony it had once held. I even noticed that I was not thinking primarily of her [though this was exactly her neighborhood], but of the appointment that I had made with someone in a restaurant nearby. I realized that Chloe's memory had neutralized itself and become a part of history. Yet guilt accompanied this forgetting. It was no longer her

absence that wounded me, but my growing indifference to it. Forgetting was a reminder of death, of loss, of infidelity to what I had at one time held so dear.

9. There was a gradual reconquering of the self, new habits were created and a Chloe-less identity built up. My identity had for so long been forged around "us" that to return to the "I" involved an almost complete reinvention of myself. It took a long time for the hundreds of associations that Chloe and I had accumulated together to fade. I had to live with my sofa for months before the image of her lying on it in her dressing gown was replaced by another image, the image of a friend reading a book on it, or of my coat lying across it. I had to walk through Islington on numberless occasions before I could forget that Islington was not simply Chloe's district, but a useful place to shop or have dinner. I had to revisit almost every physical location, rewrite over every topic of conversation, replay every song and every activity that Chloe and I had shared in order to reconquer them for the present, in order to defuse their associations. But gradually I forgot.

10. Time abbreviated itself, like an accordion that is lived in extension but remembered only in contraction. My life with Chloe was like a block of ice that was gradually melting as I carried it through the present. It was like a current event that becomes a part of history and in the process contracts into a

few central details. The process was like a film camera taking a thousand frames a minute, but discarding most of them, selecting according to mysterious whims, landing on a certain frame because an emotional state had coalesced around it. Like a century that is reduced and symbolized by a certain pope or monarch or battle, my love affair refined itself to a few iconic elements [more random than those of the historians but equally selective]: the look on Chloe's face as we kissed for the first time, the light hairs on her arm, an image of her standing waiting for me in the entrance to Liverpool Street station, what she looked like wearing her white pullover, her laugh when I told her my joke about the Russian in a train through France, her way of running her hand through her hair . . .

11. The camel became lighter and lighter as it walked through time. It kept shaking memories and photos off its back, scattering them over the desert floor and letting the wind bury them in the sand, and gradually the camel became so light that it could trot and even gallop in its own curious way—until one day, in a small oasis that called itself the present, the exhausted creature finally caught up with the rest of me.

from

MOONLIGHT
SHADOW

BANANA YOSHIMOTO

*Banana Yoshimoto's simple style takes her readers to
unexectedly profound places. In this story, a young
woman who has lost her boyfriend to a car accident
slips further and further into a kind of placid,
calm despair. Then she meets a
mysterious woman who offers her
an unexpected way to
break the spell.*

That night, as usual, I awoke from a dream of Hitoshi. I dreamed that in spite of my fever I had run to the river and Hitoshi was there. He said to me, smiling, "You've got a cold; what are you doing?" That was the lowest point yet. When I opened my eyes it was dawn, time to get up and get dressed. But it was cold, so very cold, and in spite of the fact that my whole body felt flushed, my hands and feet were like ice. I had the chills; I shuddered, my whole body in pain.

I opened my eyes, trembling in the half-darkness. I felt I was battling something absurdly enormous. Then, from deep within, I began to wonder if I mightn't lose.

It hurt to have lost Hitoshi. It hurt too much.

When we were in each other's arms, I knew something that was beyond words. It was the mystery of being close to someone who is not family. My heart dropped out, and I was feeling what people fear the most; I touched the deepest despair a person can know. I was lonely. Hideously lonely. This was the worst. If I could get through this, morning would come, and I knew without a doubt that I would have fun again, laugh out loud. If only the sun would rise. If only morning would come.

Whenever it had been like this before, I had set my teeth and stood up to it; but now, lacking the strength to go to the river, I could only suffer. Time inched along, as if I were walking on shards of glass. I felt that if I could only get to the river, Hitoshi really would be there. I felt insane. I was sick at heart.

I sluggishly got up and went to the kitchen for some tea. My throat was parched. Because of my fever, the whole house looked surreally warped, distorted; the kitchen was ice-cold and dark. Everyone was asleep. Delirious, I made tea and went back to my room.

The tea seemed to help. It soothed my dry throat and my breathing became natural again. I sat up in bed and parted the curtains.

From my room I had a good view of the front gate and yard. The trees and flowers rustled, trembling in the blue morning air—they seemed painted in flat colors, like a diorama in a museum. It was pretty. These days I was well aware of how the blue air of dawn makes everything seem purified. As I sat there peering out the window, I saw the shadow of a person coming up the sidewalk in front of my house.

I wondered if it was a dream and blinked my eyes. It was Urara. Dressed in blue, grinning broadly, she looked at me and came toward me. At the gate she mouthed, "May I come in?" I nodded. She crossed the yard and reached my window. I opened it, my heart pounding.

"Sure is cold out," she said. An icy wind came in through the window, freezing my feverish cheeks. The pure, clean air tasted delicious.

"What's up?" I asked. I must have been beaming like a happy little kid.

"I'm on my way home. Your cold is looking worse, you know. Here, I'll give you some vitamin C candy." Taking the candy from her pocket, she handed it to me, smiling artlessly.

"You're always so good to me," I said in a hoarse voice.

"You look like your temperature is very high. You must feel rotten."

"Yes," I said. "I couldn't go running this morning." For some reason I felt like crying.

"With a cold"—she spoke evenly, lowering her eyes a little—"now is the hardest time. Maybe even harder than dying. But this is probably as bad as it can get. You might come to fear the next time you get a cold; it will be as bad as this, but if you just hold steady, it won't be. For the rest of your life. That's how it works. You could take the negative view and live in fear: Will it happen again? But it won't hurt so much if you just accept it as a part of life." With that she looked up at me, smiling.

I remained silent, my eyes wide. Was she only talking about having a cold? Just what was she saying? The blue of the dawn, my fever, everything was spinning, and the boundary between dream and waking blurred. While her words were making their way into my heart, I was staring absently at her bangs, which were fluttering in the wind.

"Well, see you tomorrow." With a smile, Urara gently

shut the window from the outside. She skipped lightly out the gate.

Floating in a dream, I watched her walk away. That she had come to me at the end of a long night of misery made me want to cry tears of joy. I wanted to tell her: "How happy I am that you came to me like an apparition in that bluish mist. Now everything around me will be a little bit better when I wake up." At last I was able to fall asleep.

When I awoke I knew that my cold was at least a little better. I slept so soundly that it was evening before I woke up. I got out of bed, took a shower, put on a fresh change of clothes, started drying my hair. My fever was down and I felt quite well, except for the sensation of my body having been through the mill.

I wondered, under the hot wind of the hair dryer, if Urara had really come to see me. Maybe it was just a dream— her words resounded in my brain as if it had been. And had she really only been talking about having a cold?

My face in the mirror had a touch of dark shadow on it, making me wonder—was this a harbinger of other terrible nights to come, like the aftershocks following an earthquake? I was so tired that I couldn't bear to think about it. I was truly exhausted. But still . . . more than anything, I wanted to evade those thoughts, even if I had to do it on my hands and knees.

For one thing, I was breathing more easily than I had been even yesterday. I was sick to death at the prospect of more suffocatingly lonely nights. The idea that they would be repeated, that that was just how life was, made me shudder with horror. Still, having tasted for myself that moment when I suddenly could breathe easy again made my heart beat faster.

I found I was able to smile a little. The knowledge of how quickly my fever had dissipated made me a little giddy. Just then there was an unexpected knock at my bedroom door. I thought it was my mother and said, "Come in." When the door opened, I was amazed to see Hiiragi.

"Your mother says she kept calling you, but you didn't answer," he said.

"I was drying my hair, I guess I couldn't hear." I was embarrassed to be caught in the intimacy of my room with just-washed, unstyled hair, but he said, nonplussed, "When I phoned, your mother said you had a cold, like a terrible teething fever, so I thought I'd come and see how you're doing."

I remembered that he'd been here with Hitoshi, like the day of the festival and that time after the baseball game. So, just like old times, he grabbed a cushion and flopped down. It was only I who had forgotten how well we knew each other.

"I brought you a get-well present." Hiiragi laughed, indicating a large paper bag. At this point I couldn't tell him I was actually just about over it. I even forced a cough. He had come all this way because he thought I was sick. "It's a chicken filet sandwich from Kentucky Fried, which I know you love, and some sherbet. Cokes, too. And, I brought enough for myself, so let's eat."

He was treating me like I was made of brittle glass. My mother must have said something to him. I was embarrassed. Still, it wasn't as if I were so much better I could say flat out, "I'm completely well!"

In the brightly lit room, warmed by my little heater, the two of us calmly ate what he had brought. The food was delicious, and I realized how very, very hungry I was. It occurred to me I always enjoyed what I ate when I was with him. How wonderful that is, I thought.

"Satsuki."

"What?" In a reverie, realizing he had said my name, I looked up.

"You've got to stop torturing yourself, all alone, getting thinner and thinner—you even got a fever from it. When you feel like that, call me up. We'll get together, go do something. Every time I see you you look more frail, but you pretend everything's all right. That's a waste of energy. I know you and Hitoshi were so happy together that now you could die of sadness. It's only natural."

He had never said anything like that. It was odd—that was the first time I had seen him express such emotion: sympathy as open and unguarded as a child's. Because I had thought his style too cool for that, it was totally unexpected, this purehearted concern. But then I remembered Hitoshi saying how Hiiragi, usually old beyond his years, reverted to a childlike state where the family was concerned. I had to smile—I felt I understood now what Hitoshi had meant.

"I know I'm still a kid, and when I take off the sailor outfit I feel so alone I could cry, but we're all brothers and sisters when we're in trouble, aren't we? I care about you so much, I just want to crawl into the same bed with you."

He said it with such an utterly sincere face, and it was so obvious his intentions were honorable, I had to smile in spite of myself. Then I said to him, deeply moved, "I'll do as you say. I really will, I'll call you, I mean it. Thank you. Really, truly, thank you."

After Hiiragi left I went back to sleep. Thanks to the cold medicine I took, I slept through a long, peaceful, dreamless night. It was the divine, anticipatory sleep I remember having slept as a child on Christmas Eve. When I awoke, I would go to Urara waiting at the river, and I would see the "something."

It was before dawn. Although my health was not quite back to normal, I got dressed and went running. It was the kind of frozen morning in which moon shadows seem to be pasted on the sky. The sound of my footsteps resonated in the silent blue air and faded away into the emptiness of the streets.

Urara was standing by the bridge. When I got there her hands were in her pockets and her muffler covered her mouth, but her sparkling eyes showed she was smiling brightly. "Good morning," she said.

The last few stars in the blue porcelain sky winked, a dim white, as if about to go out. The scene was thrillingly beautiful. The river roared furiously; the air was very clear.

"So blue it feels like it could melt right into your body," said Urara, gesturing at the sky.

The faint outline of the rustling trees trembled in the wind; gently, the heavens began to move. The moon shone through the half-dark.

"It's time." Urara's voice was tense. "Ready? What's going to happen next is, the dimension we're in—time, space, all that stuff—is going to move, shift a little. You and I, although we'll be standing side by side, probably won't be able to see each other, and we won't be seeing the same things . . . across the river. Whatever you do, you mustn't say anything, and you mustn't cross the bridge. Got it?"

I nodded. "Got it."

• • •

Then we fell silent. The only sound the roaring of the river, side by side Urara and I fixed our eyes on the far bank. My heart was pounding. I realized my legs were trembling. Dawn crept up little by little. The sky changed to a light blue. The birds began to sing.

I had a feeling that I heard something faint, far away. I looked to one side and was startled—Urara wasn't there anymore. The river, myself, the sky—then, blended with the sounds of the wind and the river, I heard what I'd longed for.

A bell. There was no question, it was Hitoshi's. The sound came, faintly tinkling, from a spot where no one was standing. I closed my eyes, making sure of the sound. Then I opened them, and when I looked across the river I felt crazier than I had in the whole last two months. I just barely managed to keep from crying out.

There was Hitoshi.

Across the river, if this wasn't a dream, and I wasn't crazy, the figure facing me was Hitoshi. Separated from him by the water, my chest welling up, I focused my eyes on that form, the very image of the memory I kept in my heart.

Through the blue haze, he was looking in my direction. He had that worried expression he always had when I acted recklessly. His hands in his pockets, his eyes found mine. The years I had spent in his arms seemed both very near and very far away. We simply gazed at each other. Only the fading moon saw the too-violent current, the too-distant chasm between us. My hair, the collar of Hitoshi's dear, familiar shirt fluttered in the wind off the river as softly as in a dream.

Hitoshi, do you want to talk to me? I want to talk to you. I want to run to your side, take you in my arms, and rejoice in being together again. But, but—the tears flowed—fate has decided that you and I be so clearly divided like this, facing each other across the river, and I don't have a say in it.

My tears fell like rain; all I could do was stare at him. Hitoshi looked sadly back at me. I wished time could stop—but with the first rays of the rising sun everything slowly began to fade away. Before my eyes, Hitoshi grew faint. When I began to panic, he smiled and waved his hand. Again and again, he waved his hand. He was disappearing into the blue void. I, too, waved. Dear, much missed Hitoshi—I tried to burn the line of his dear shoulders, his dear arms, all of him, into my brain. The faint colors of his form, even the heat of the tears running down my cheeks: I desperately struggled to memorize it all. The arching lines described by his arm remained, like an after-image, suspended in the air. His form was slowly growing fainter, disappearing. I stared at it through my tears.

By the time I could no longer see anything at all, everything had returned to normal: morning by the river. I looked to one side; there stood Urara. Still facing straight ahead, a heart-breaking sadness in her eyes, she asked me, "Did you see it?"

"Yes," I said, wiping away my tears.

"Was it everything you had hoped?" This time she

turned to face me, smiling. Relief diffused through my heart. "It was," I said, smiling back at her. The two of us stood there in the sunshine for some time, as morning came.

The doughnut shop had just opened. Urara, her eyes a little sleepy, said over a hot cup of coffee, "I came to this place because I, too, lost my lover to an early death. I came hoping to say a last good-bye."

"Were you able to?" I asked.

"Yes." Urara smiled a little. "It really does happen only once every hundred years or so, and then only if a number of chance factors happen to line up right. The time and the place are not definitely set. People who know about it call it 'The Weaver Festival Phenomenon.' It can only take place near a large river. Some people can't see it at all. The residual thoughts of a person who has died meet the sadness of someone left behind, and the vision is produced. This was my first experience of it, too . . . . I think you were very lucky today."

"Every hundred years . . ." My mind raced at the thought of the probabilities involved in my having been able to see it.

"When I arrived here to take a preliminary look at the site, there you were. My animal instincts told me that you had lost someone yourself. That's why I invited you." The morning sun shone through her hair. Urara, smiling, was still as a statue while she spoke.

What kind of person was she, really? Where had she come from and where would she go from here? And who had she seen across the river? I couldn't ask her.

"Parting and death are both terribly painful. But to keep nursing the memory of a love so great you can't believe you'll ever love again is a useless drain on a woman's energies." Urara spoke through a mouthful of doughnut, as if making casual chitchat.

"So I think it's for the best that we were able to say a proper, final good-bye today." Her eyes became terribly sad.

". . . Yes," I said. "So do I." Urara's eyes narrowed gently as she sat in the sunlight.

Hitoshi waving good-bye. It was a painful sight, like a ray of light piercing my heart.

Whether it had been for the best was not something I as yet fully understood. I only knew that, right now, sitting in the strong sunlight, its lingering memory in my breast was very painful. It hurt so much I could barely breathe.

Still . . . still, looking at the smiling Urara before me, amid the smell of weak coffee, the feeling was strong within me of having been very near the "something." I heard the windows rattle in the wind. Like Hitoshi when we parted, no matter how much I could lay bare my heart, no matter how much I strained my eyes, that "something" would remain transitory. That was certain. That "something" shone in the gloom with the strength of the sun itself; at a great speed, I was coming through. In a downpour of blessings, I prayed, as though it were a hymn: Let me become stronger.

"Where will you go now?" I asked as we walked out of the doughnut shop.

Smiling, she took my hand. "We'll meet again someday. I'll never forget your phone number."

With that, she melted into the wave of people crowding the morning streets. I watched her go and thought, I, too, will not forget. How very much you have given me.

A LETTER THAT NEVER REACHED RUSSIA

VLADIMIR NABOKOV

*In this story, an exile from Stalinist Russia writes to
the "charming, dear, distant one" whom he will never
see again, capturing the romance of solitary yearning
in his evocative descriptions of "everything with
which God so generously surrounds
you in loneliness."*

My charming, dear, distant one, I presume you cannot have forgotten anything in the more than eight years of our separation, if you manage to remember even the gray-haired, azure-liveried watchman who did not bother us in the least when we would meet, skipping school, on a frosty Petersburg morning, in the Suvorov Museum, so dusty, so small, so similar to a glorified snuffbox. How ardently we kissed behind a waxen grenadier's back! And later, when we came out of that antique dust, how dazzled we were by the silvery blaze of the Tavricheski Park, and how odd it was to hear the cheery, avid, deep-fetched grunts of soldiers, lunging on command, slithering across the icy ground, plunging a bayonet into the straw-bellied German-helmeted dummy in the middle of a Petersburg street.

Yes, I know that I had sworn, in my previous letter to you, not to mention the past, especially the trifles in our shared past; for we authors in exile are supposed to possess a lofty pudicity of expression, and yet, here I am, from the very first lines, disdaining that right to sublime imperfection, and defeating with epithets the recollection on which you touched with such lightness and grace. Not of the past, my love, do I wish to speak to you.

It is night. At night one perceives with a special intensity the immobility of objects—the lamp, the furniture, the framed photographs on one's desk. Now and then the water gulps and gurgles in its hidden pipes as if sobs were rising to the throat of the house. At night I go out for a stroll. Reflections of streetlamps trickle across the damp Berlin asphalt whose surface resembles a film of black grease with puddles nestling in its wrinkles. Here and there a garnet-red light glows over a fire-alarm box. A glass column, full of liquid yellow light, stands at the streetcar stop, and, for some reason, I get such a blissful, melancholy sensation when, late at night, its wheels screeching around the bend, a tram hurtles past, empty. Through its windows one can clearly see the rows of brightly lit brown seats between which a lone ticket collector with a black satchel at his side makes his way, reeling a bit and thus looking a little tight—as he moves against the direction of the car's travel.

As I wander along some silent, dark street, I like to hear a man coming home. The man himself is not visible in the darkness, and you never know beforehand which front door will come alive to accept a key with grinding condescension, swing open, pause, retained by the counterweight, slam shut; the key will grind again from the inside, and, in the depths beyond the glass pane of the door, a soft radiance will linger for one marvelous minute.

A car rolls by on pillars of wet light. It is black, with a yellow stripe beneath the windows. It trumpets gruffly into the ear of the night, and its shadow passes under my feet. By now the street is totally deserted—except for an aged Great Dane whose claws rap on the sidewalk as it reluctantly takes for a walk a listless, pretty, hatless girl with an opened umbrella. When she passes under the garnet bulb (on her left, above the fire alarm), a single taut, black segment of her umbrella reddens damply.

And beyond the bend, above the sidewalk—how unexpectedly!—the front of a cinema ripples in diamonds. Inside, on its rectangular, moon-pale screen you can watch more-or-less skillfully trained mimes: the huge face of a girl with gray, shimmering eyes and black lips traversed vertically by glistening cracks, approaches from the screen, keeps growing as it gazes into the dark hall, and a wonderful, long, shining tear runs down one cheek. And occasionally (a heavenly moment!) there appears real life, unaware that it is being filmed: a chance crowd, bright waters, a noiselessly but visibly rustling tree.

Farther on, at the corner of a square, a stout prostitute in black furs slowly walks to and fro, stopping occasionally in front of a harshly lighted shop window where a rouged woman of wax shows off to night wanderers her streamy, emerald gown and the shiny silk of her peach-colored stockings. I like to observe this placid middle-aged whore, as she is approached by an elderly man with a mustache, who came on business that morning from Papenburg (first he passes her and takes two backward glances). She will conduct him unhurriedly to a room in a nearby building, which, in the daytime, is quite undistinguishable from other, equally ordinary buildings. A polite and impassive old porter keeps an all-night vigil in the unlighted front hall. At the top of a steep staircase an equally impassive old woman will unlock with sage unconcern an unoccupied room and receive payment for it.

And do you know with what a marvelous clatter the brightly lit train, all its windows laughing, sweeps across the bridge above the street! Probably it goes no farther than the suburbs, but in that instant the darkness beneath the black span of the bridge is filled with such mighty metallic music that I cannot help imagining the sunny lands toward which I shall depart as soon as I have procured those extra hundred marks for which I long so blandly, so lightheartedly.

I am so lighthearted that sometimes I even enjoy watching people dancing in the local café. Many fellow exiles of mine denounce indignantly (and in this indignation there is a pinch of pleasure) fashionable abominations, including current dances. But fashion is a creature of man's mediocrity, a certain level of life, the vulgarity of equality, and to denounce it means admitting that mediocrity can create something (whether it be a form of government or a new kind of hairdo) worth making a fuss about. And of course these so-called modern dances of ours are actually anything but modern: the craze goes back to the days of the Directoire, for then as now women's dresses were worn next to the skin, and the musicians were Negroes. Fashion breathes through the centuries: the dome-shaped crinoline of the middle 1800s was the full inhalation of fashion's breath, followed by exhalation: narrowing skirts, close dances. Our dances, after all, are very natural and pretty innocent, and sometimes—in London ballrooms—perfectly graceful in their monotony. We all remember what Pushkin wrote about the waltz: "monotonous and mad." It's all the same thing. As for the deterioration of morals . . . Here's what I found in D'Agricourt's memoirs: "I know nothing more depraved than the minuet, which they see fit to dance in our cities."

And so I enjoy watching, in the *cafés dansants* here, how "pair after pair flick by," to quote Pushkin again. Amusingly made-up eyes sparkle with simple human merriment. Black-trousered and light-stockinged legs touch. Feet turn this way and that. And meanwhile, outside the door, waits my faithful, my lonely night with its moist reflections, hooting cars, and gusts of high-blowing wind.

On that kind of night, at the Russian Orthodox cemetery far outside the city, an old lady of seventy committed suicide on the grave of her recently deceased husband. I happened to go there the next morning, and the watchman, a badly crippled veteran of the Denikin campaign, moving on crutches that creaked with every swing of his body, showed me the white cross on which she hanged herself, and the yellow strands still adhering where the rope ("brand-new one," he said gently) had chafed. Most mysterious and enchanting of all, though, were the crescent-shaped prints left by her heels, tiny as a child's, on the damp soil by the plinth. "She trampled the ground a bit, poor thing, but apart from that there's no mess at all," observed the watchman calmly, and, glancing at those yellow strands and at those little depressions, I suddenly realized that one can distinguish a naive smile even in death. Possibly, dear, my main reason for writing this letter is to tell you of that easy, gentle end. Thus the Berlin night resolved itself.

Listen: I am ideally happy. My happiness is a kind of challenge. As I wander along the streets and the squares and the paths by the canal, absently sensing the lips of dampness through my worn soles, I carry proudly my ineffable happiness. The centuries will roll by, and schoolboys will yawn over the history of our upheavals; everything will pass, but my happiness, dear, my happiness will remain, in the moist reflection of a streetlamp, in the cautious bend of stone steps that descend into the canal's black waters, in the smiles of a dancing couple, in everything with which God so generously surrounds human loneliness.

D U L S E

ALICE MUNRO

Sometimes new love itself is not needed, but merely the suggestion of new love. The heroine of Munro's story finds that even subtle—and unwanted—advances from a perfect stranger can put a failed relationship in a whole new light.

At the end of the summer Lydia took a boat to an island off the southern coast of New Brunswick, where she was going to stay overnight. She had just a few days left until she had to be back in Ontario. She worked as an editor, for a publisher in Toronto. She was also a poet, but she did not refer to that unless it was something people knew already. For the past eighteen months she had been living with a man in Kingston. As far as she could see, that was over.

She had noticed something about herself on this trip to the Maritimes. It was that people were no longer so interested in getting to know her. It wasn't that she had created such a stir before, but something had been there that she could rely on. She was forty-five, and had been divorced for nine years. Her two children had started on their own lives, though there were still retreats and confusions. She hadn't got fatter or thinner, her looks had not deteriorated in any alarming way, but nevertheless she had stopped being one sort of woman and had become another, and she had noticed it on this trip. She was not surprised because she was in a new, strange condition at the time. She made efforts, one after the other. She set little blocks on top of one another and she had a day. Sometimes she almost could not do this. At other times the very deliberateness, the seeming arbitrariness, of what she was doing, the way she was living, exhilarated her.

She found a guesthouse overlooking the docks, with their stacks of lobster traps, and the few scattered stores and houses that made up the village. A woman of about her own age was cooking dinner. This woman took her to a cheap, old-fashioned room upstairs. There were no other guests around, though the room next door was open and seemed to be occupied, perhaps by a child. Whoever it was had left several comic books on the floor beside the bed.

She went for a walk up the steep lane behind the guest-house. She occupied herself by naming shrubs and weeds. The goldenrod and wild aster were in bloom, and Japanese boxwood, a rarity in Ontario, seemed commonplace here. The grass was long and coarse and the trees were small. The Atlantic coast, which she had never seen before, was just as she had expected it to be. The bending grass; the bare houses; the sea light. She started wondering what it would be like to live there, whether the houses were still cheap or if people from the outside had started to buy them up. Often on this trip she had busied herself with calculations of this kind, and also with ideas of how she could make a living in some new way, cut off from everything she had done before. She did not think of making a living writing poetry, not only because the income would be so low but because she thought, as she had thought innumerable times in her life, that probably she would not write any more poems. She was thinking that she could not cook well enough to do it for pay but she could clean. There was at least one other guesthouse besides the one where she was staying, and she had seen a sign advertising a motel. How many hours' cleaning could she get if she cleaned all three places, and how much an hour did cleaning pay?

There were four small tables in the dining room, but only one man was sitting there, drinking tomato juice. He did not look at her. A man who was probably the husband of the woman she had met earlier came in from the kitchen. He had a grayish-blond beard, and a downcast look. He asked Lydia's name and took her to the table where the man was sitting. The man stood up, stiffly, and Lydia was introduced. The man's name was Mr. Stanley and Lydia took him to be about sixty. Politely, he asked her to sit down.

Three men in work clothes came in and sat down at another table. They were not noisy in any self-important or offensive way, but just coming in and disposing themselves around the table, they created an enjoyable commotion. That is, they enjoyed it, and looked as if they expected others to. Mr. Stanley bowed in their direction. It really was a little bow, not just a nod of the head. He said good evening. They asked him what there was for supper, and he said he believed it was scallops, with pumpkin pie for dessert.

"These gentlemen work for the New Brunswick Telephone Company," he said to Lydia. "They are laying a cable to one of the smaller islands, and they stay here during the week."

He was older than she had thought at first. It did not show in his voice, which was precise and American, or in the movements of his hands, but in his small, separate, brownish teeth, and in his eyes, which had a delicate milky skin over the light-brown iris.

The husband brought their food, and spoke to the workmen. He was an efficient waiter, but rather stiff and remote, rather like a sleepwalker, in fact, as if he did not perform this job in his real life. The vegetables were served in large bowls, from which they helped themselves. Lydia was glad to see so much food: broccoli, mashed turnips, potatoes, corn. The American took small helpings of everything and began to eat in a very deliberate way, giving the impression that the order in which he lifted forkfuls of food to his mouth was not haphazard, that there was a reason for the turnip to follow the potatoes, and for the deep-fried scallops, which were not large, to be cut neatly in half. He looked up a couple of times as if he thought of saying something, but he did not do it. The workmen were quiet now too, laying into the food.

Mr. Stanley spoke at last. He said, "Are you familiar with the writer Willa Cather?"

"Yes." Lydia was startled, because she had not seen anybody reading a book for the past two weeks; she had not even noticed any paperback racks.

"Do you know, then, that she spent every summer here?"

"Here?"

"On this island. She had her summer home here. Not more than a mile away from where we are sitting now. She came here for eighteen years, and she wrote many of her books here. She wrote in a room that had a view of the sea, but now the trees have grown up and blocked it. She was with her great friend, Edith Lewis. Have you read *A Lost Lady*?"

Lydia said that she had.

"It is my favorite of all her books. She wrote it here. At least, she wrote a great part of it here."

Lydia was aware of the workmen listening, although they did not glance up from their food. She felt that even without looking at Mr. Stanley or each other they might manage to communicate an indulgent contempt. She thought she did not care whether or not she was included in this contempt, but perhaps it was for that reason that she did not find anything much to say about Willa Cather, or tell Mr. Stanley that she worked for a publisher, let alone that she was any sort of writer herself. Or it could have been just that Mr. Stanley did not give her much of a chance.

"I have been her admirer for over sixty years," he said. He paused, holding his knife and fork over his plate. "I read and reread her, and my admiration grows. It simply grows. There are people here who remember her. Tonight, I am going to see a woman, a woman who knew Willa, and had conversations with her. She is eighty-eight years old but they say she has not forgotten. The people here are beginning to learn of my interest and they will remember someone like this and put me in touch.

"It is a great delight to me," he said solemnly.

All the time he was talking, Lydia was trying to think what his conversational style reminded her of. It didn't remind her of any special person, though she might have had one or two teachers at college who talked like that. What it made her think of was a time when a few people, just a few people, had never concerned themselves with being democratic, or ingratiating, in their speech; they spoke in formal, well-thought-out, slightly self-congratulating sentences, though they lived in a country where their formality, their pedantry, could bring them nothing but mockery. No, that was not the whole truth. It brought mockery, and an uncomfortable admiration. What he made Lydia think of, really, was the old-fashioned culture of provincial cities long ago (something she of course had never known, but sensed from books); the high-mindedness, the propriety; hard plush concert seats and hushed libraries. And his adoration of the chosen writer was of a piece with this; it was just as out-of-date as his speech. She thought that he could not be a teacher; such worship was not in style for teachers, even of his age.

"Do you teach literature?"

"No. Oh, no. I have not had that privilege. No. I have not even studied literature. I went to work when I was sixteen. In my day there was not so much choice. I have worked on newspapers."

She thought of some absurdly discreet and conservative New England paper with a fusty prose style.

"Oh. Which paper?" she said, then realized her inquisitiveness must seem quite rude, to anyone so circumspect.

"Not a paper you would have heard of. Just the daily paper of an industrial town. Other papers in the earlier years. That was my life."

"And now, would you like to do a book on Willa Cather?" This question seemed not so out of place to her, because she was always talking to people who wanted to do books about something.

"No," he said austerely. "My eyes do not permit me to do any reading or writing beyond what is necessary."

That was why he was so deliberate about his eating.

"No," he went on, "I don't say that at one time I might not have thought of that, doing a book on Willa. I would have written something just about her life here on the island. Biographies have been done, but not so much on that phase of her life. Now I have given up the idea. I do my investigating just for my own pleasure. I take a camp chair up there, so I can sit underneath the window where she wrote and looked at the sea. There is never anybody there."

"It isn't being kept up? It isn't any sort of memorial?"

"Oh, no indeed. It isn't kept up at all. The people here, you know, while they were very impressed with Willa, and some of them recognized her genius—I mean the genius of her personality, for they would not be able to recognize the genius of her work—others of them thought her unfriendly and did not like her. They took offense because she was unsociable, as she had to be, to do her writing."

"It could be a project," Lydia said. "Perhaps they could get some money from the government. The Canadian government and the Americans too. They could preserve the house."

"Well, that isn't for me to say." He smiled; he shook his head. "I don't think so. No."

He did not want any other worshippers coming to disturb him in his camp chair. She should have known that. What would this private pilgrimage of his be worth if other people got into the act, and signs were put up, leaflets printed; if this guesthouse, which was now called Sea View, had to be renamed Shadows on the Rock? He would let the house fall down and the grass grow over it sooner than see that.

After Lydia's last attempt to call Duncan, the man she had been living with in Kingston, she had walked along the street in Toronto, knowing that she had to get to the bank, she had to buy some food, she had to get on the subway. She had to remember directions, and the order in which to do things: to open her checkbook, to move forward when it was her turn in line, to choose one kind of bread over another, to drop a token in the slot. These seemed to be the most difficult things she had ever done. She had immense difficulty reading the names of the subway stations, and getting off at the right one, so that she could go to the apartment where she was staying. She would have found it hard to describe this difficulty. She knew perfectly well which was the right stop, she knew which stop it came after; she knew where she was. But she could not make the connection between herself and things outside herself, so that getting up and leaving the car, going up the steps, going along the street all seemed to involve a bizarre effort. She thought afterwards that she had been seized up, as machines are said to be. Even at the time she had an image of herself. She saw herself as something like an egg carton, hollowed out in back.

When she reached the apartment she sat down on a chair in the hall. She sat for an hour or so; then she went to the bathroom, undressed, put on her nightgown, and got into bed. In bed she felt triumph and relief, that she had managed all the difficulties and got herself to where she was supposed to be and would not have to remember anything more.

She didn't feel at all like committing suicide. She couldn't have managed the implements, or aids, she couldn't even have thought which to use. It amazed her to think that she had chosen the loaf of bread and the cheese, which were now lying on the floor in the hall. How had she imagined she was going to chew and swallow them?

• • •

After dinner Lydia sat out on the veranda with the woman who had cooked the meal. The woman's husband did the cleaning up.

"Well, of course we have a dishwasher," the woman said. "We have two freezers and an oversized refrigerator. You have to make an investment. You get the crews staying with you, you have to feed them. This place soaks up money like a sponge. We're going to put in a swimming pool next year. We need more attractions. You have to run to stay in the same place. People think what an easy nice life. Boy."

She had a strong, lined face, and long straight hair. She wore jeans and an embroidered smock and a man's sweater.

"Ten years ago I was living in a commune in the States. Now I'm here. I work sometimes eighteen hours a day. I have to pack the crew's lunch yet tonight. I cook and bake, cook and bake. John does the rest."

"Do you have someone to clean?"

"We can't afford to hire anybody. John does it. He does the laundry—everything. We had to buy a mangle for the sheets. We had to put in a new furnace. We got a bank loan. I thought that was funny, because I used to be married to a bank manager. I left him."

"I'm on my own now too."

"Are you? You can't be on your own forever. I met John, and he was in the same boat."

"I was living with a man in Kingston, in Ontario."

"Were you? John and I are extremely happy. He used to be a minister. But when I met him he was doing carpentry. We both had sort of dropped out. Did you talk to Mr. Stanley?"

"Yes."

"Had you ever heard of Willa Cather?"

"Yes."

"That'd make him happy. I don't read hardly at all, it doesn't mean anything to me. I'm a visual person. But I think he's a wonderful character, old Mr. Stanley. He's a real old scholar."

"Has he been coming here for a long time?"

"No, he hasn't. This is just his third year. He says he's wanted to come here all his life. But he couldn't. He had to wait till some relative died, that he was looking after. Not a wife. A brother, maybe. Anyway he had to wait. How old do you think he is?"

"Seventy? Seventy-five?"

"That man is eighty-one. Isn't that amazing? I really admire people like that. I really do. I admire people that keep going."

"The man I was living with—that is, the man I used to live with, in Kingston," said Lydia, "was putting some boxes of papers in the trunk of his car once, this was out in the country, at an old farmhouse, and he felt something nudge him and he glanced down. It was about dusk, on a pretty dark day. So he thought this was a big friendly dog, a big black dog giving him a nudge, and he didn't pay much attention. He just said go on, now, boy, go away now, good boy. Then when he got the boxes arranged he turned around. And he saw it was a bear. It was a black bear."

She was telling this later that same evening, in the kitchen.

"So what did he do then?" said Lawrence, who was the boss of the telephone work crew. Lawrence and Lydia and Eugene and Vincent were playing cards.

Lydia laughed. "He said, *Excuse me*. That's what he claims he said."

"Papers all he had in the boxes? Nothing to eat?"

"He's a writer. He writes historical books. This was some material he needed for his work. Sometimes he has to go and scout out material from people who are very strange. That bear hadn't come out of the bush. It was a pet, actually, that had been let off its chain, for a joke. There were two old brothers there, that he got the papers from, and they just let it off its chain to give him a scare."

"That's what he does, collects old stuff and writes about it?" Lawrence said. "I guess that's interesting."

She immediately regretted having told this story. She had brought it up because the men were talking about bears. But there wasn't much point to it unless Duncan told it. He could show you himself, large and benign and civilized, with his courtly apologies to the bear. He could make you see the devilish old men behind their tattered curtains.

"You'd have to know Duncan" was what she almost said. And hadn't she told this simply to establish that she had known Duncan—that she had recently had a man, and an interesting man, an amusing and adventurous man? She wanted to assure them that she was not always alone, going on her aimless travels. She had to show herself attached. A mistake. They were not likely to think a man adventurous who collected old papers from misers and eccentrics, so that he could write books about things that had happened a hundred years ago. She shouldn't even have said that Duncan was a man she had lived with. All that could mean, to them, was that she was a woman who had slept with a man she was not married to.

Lawrence the boss was not yet forty, but he was successful. He was glad to tell about himself. He was a free-lance labor contractor and owned two houses in St. Stephen. He had two cars and a truck and a boat. His wife taught school. Lawrence was getting a thick waist, a trucker's belly, but he still looked alert and vigorous. You could see that he would be shrewd enough, in most situations, for his purposes; sure enough, ruthless enough. Dressed up, he might turn flashy. And certain places and people might be capable of making him gloomy, uncertain, contentious.

Lawrence said it wasn't all true—all the stuff they wrote about the Maritimes. He said there was plenty of work for people who weren't afraid to work. Men or women. He said he was not against women's lib, but the fact was, and always would be, that there was work men did better than women and work women did better than men, and if they would both settle down and realize that they'd be happier.

His kids were cheeky, he said. They had it too soft. They got everything—that was the way nowadays, what could you do? The other kids got everything too. Clothes, bikes, education, records. He hadn't had anything handed to him. He had got out and worked, driven trucks. He had got to Ontario, got as far as Saskatchewan. He had only got to Grade 10 in school but he hadn't let that hold him back. Sometimes he wished, though, that he did have more of an education.

Eugene and Vincent, who worked for Lawrence, said they had never got past Grade 8, when that was as far as you could go in the country schools. Eugene was twenty-five and Vincent was fifty-two. Eugene was French-Canadian from northern New Brunswick. He looked younger than his age. He had a rosy color, a downy, dreamy look—a masculine beauty that was nevertheless soft-edged, sweet-tempered, bashful. Hardly any men or boys have that look nowadays. Sometimes you see it in an old photograph—of a bridegroom, a basketball player: the thick water-combed hair, the blooming boy's face on the new man's body. Eugene was not very bright, or perhaps not very competitive. He lost money at the game they were playing. It was a card game that the men called Skat. Lydia remembered playing it when she was a child, and calling it Thirty-one. They played for a quarter a game.

Eugene permitted Vincent and Lawrence to tease him about losing at cards, about getting lost in St. John, about women he liked, and about being French-Canadian. Lawrence's teasing amounted to bullying. Lawrence wore a carefully, good-natured expression, but he looked as if something hard and heavy had settled inside him—a load of self-esteem that weighed him down instead of buoying him up. Vincent had no such extra weight, and though he too was relentless in his teasing—he teased Lawrence as well as Eugene—there was no sense of cruelty or danger. You could see that his natural tone was one of rumbling, easy mockery. He was sharp and sly but not insistent; he would always be able to say the most pessimistic things and not sound unhappy.

Vincent had a farm—it was his family's farm, where he had grown up, near St. Stephen. He said you couldn't make enough to keep you nowadays, just from farming. Last year he put in a potato crop. There was frost in June, snow in September. Too short a season by a long shot. You never knew, he said, when you might get it like that. And the market is all controlled now; it is all run by the big fellows, the big interests. Everybody does what he can, rather than trust to farming. Vincent's wife works too. She took a course and learned to do hair. His sons are not hard-working like their parents. All they want to do is roar around in cars. They get married and the first thing their wives want is a new stove. They want a stove that practically cooks the dinner by itself and puts it on the table.

It didn't use to be that way. The first time Vincent ever had boots of his own—new boots that hadn't been worn by anybody before him—was when he joined the army. He was so pleased he walked backwards in the dirt to see the prints they made, fresh and whole. Later on, after the war, he went to St. John to look for work. He had been working at home on the farm for a while and he had worn out his army clothes—he had just one pair of decent pants left. In a beer parlor in St. John a man said to him, "You want to pick up a good pair of pants cheap?" Vincent said yes, and the man said, "Follow me." So Vincent did. And where did they end up? At the undertaker's! For the fact was that the family of a dead man usually bring in a suit of clothes to dress him in, and he only needs to be dressed from the waist up, that's all that shows in the coffin. The undertaker sold the pants. That was true. The army gave Vincent his first pair of new boots and a corpse donated the best pair of pants he ever wore, up to that time.

Vincent had no teeth. This was immediately apparent, but it did not make him look unattractive; it simply deepened his look of secrecy and humor. His face was long and his chin tucked in, his glance unchallenging but unfooled. He was a lean man, with useful muscles, and graying black hair. You could see all the years of hard work on him, and some years of it ahead, and the body just equal to it until he turned into a ropy-armed old man, shrunken, uncomplaining, hanging on to a few jokes.

While they played Skat the talk was boisterous and interrupted all the time by exclamations, joking threats to do with the game, laughter. Afterwards it became more serious and personal. They had been drinking a local beer called Moose, but when the game was over Lawrence went out to the truck and brought in some Ontario beer, thought to be better. They called it "the imported stuff." The couple who owned the guesthouse had long ago gone to bed, but the workmen and Lydia sat on in the kitchen, just as if it belonged to one of them, drinking beer and eating dulse, which Vincent had brought down from his room. Dulse was a kind of seaweed, greenish brown, salty and fishy-tasting. Vincent said it was what he ate last thing at night and first thing in the morning— nothing could beat it. Now that they had found out it was so good for you, they sold it in the stores, done up in little wee packages at a criminal price.

The next day was Friday, and the men would be leaving the island for the mainland. They talked about trying to get the two-thirty boat instead of the one they usually caught, at five-thirty, because the forecast was for rough weather; the tail end of one of the tropical hurricanes was due to hit the Bay of Fundy before night.

"But the ferries won't run if it's too rough, will they?" said Lydia. "They won't run if it's dangerous?" She thought that she would not mind being cut off, she wouldn't mind not having to travel again in the morning.

"Well, there's a lot of fellows waiting to get off the island on a Friday night," Vincent said.

"Wanting to get home to their wives," said Lawrence sardonically. "There's always crews working over here, always men away from home." Then he began to talk in an unhurried but insistent way about sex. He talked about what he called the immorality on the island. He said that at one time the authorities had been going to put a quarantine around the whole island, on account of the V.D. Crews came over here to work and stayed at the motel, the Ocean Wave, and there'd be parties there all night every night, with drinking and young girls turning up offering themselves for sale. Girls fourteen and fifteen—oh, thirteen years of age. On the island, he said, it was getting so a woman of twenty-five could practically be a grandmother. The place was famous. Those girls would do anything for a price, sometimes for a beer.

"And sometimes for nothing," said Lawrence. He luxuriated in the telling.

They heard the front door open.

"Your old boyfriend," Lawrence said to Lydia.

She was bewildered for a moment, thinking of Duncan.

"The old fellow at the table," said Vincent.

Mr. Stanley did not come into the kitchen. He crossed the living room and climbed the stairs.

"Hey? Been down to the Ocean Wave?" said Lawrence softly, raising his head as if to call through the ceiling. "Old bugger wouldn't know what to do with it," he said. "Wouldn't've known fifty years ago any better than now. I don't let any of my crews go near that place. Do I, Eugene?"

Eugene blushed. He put on a solemn expression, as if he was being badgered by a teacher at school.

"Eugene, now, he don't have to," Vincent said.

"Isn't it true what I'm saying?" said Lawrence urgently, as if somebody had been disputing with him. "It's true, isn't it?"

He looked at Vincent, and Vincent said, "Yeah. Yeah." He did not seem to relish the subject as much as Lawrence did.

"You'd think it was all so innocent here," said Lawrence to Lydia. "Innocent! Oh, boy!"

Lydia went upstairs to get a quarter that she owed Lawrence from the last game. When she came out of her room into the dark hall, Eugene was standing there, looking out the window.

"I hope it don't storm too bad," he said.

Lydia stood beside him, looking out. The moon was visible, but misty.

"You didn't grow up near the water?" she said.

"No, I didn't."

"But if you get the two-thirty boat it'll be all right, won't it?"

"I sure hope so." He was quite childlike and unembarrassed about his fear. "One thing I don't like the idea of is getting drownded."

Lydia remembered that as a child she had said "drownded." Most of the adults and all the children she knew then said that.

"You won't," she said, in a firm, maternal way. She went downstairs and paid her quarter.

"Where's Eugene?" Lawrence said. "He upstairs?"

"He's looking out the window. He's worried about the storm."

Lawrence laughed. "You tell him to go to bed and forget about it. He's right in the room next to you. I just thought you ought to know in case he hollers in his sleep."

Lydia had first seen Duncan in a bookstore, where her friend Warren worked. She was waiting for Warren to go out to lunch with her. He had gone to get his coat. A man asked Shirley, the other clerk in the store, if she could find him a copy of *Persian Letters*. That was Duncan. Shirley walked ahead of him to where the book was kept, and in the quiet store Lydia heard him saying that it must be difficult to know where to shelve *Persian Letters*. Should it be classed as fiction or as a political essay? Lydia felt that he revealed something, saying this. He revealed a need that she supposed was common to customers in the bookstore, a need to distinguish himself, appear knowledgeable. Later on she would look back on this moment and try to imagine him again so powerless, slightly ingratiating, showing a bit of neediness. Warren came back with his coat on, greeted Duncan, and as he and Lydia went outside Warren said under his breath, "The Tin Woodman." Warren and Shirley livened up their days with nicknames for customers; Lydia had already heard of Marble-Mouth, and Chickpea and the Colonial Duchess. Duncan was the Tin Woodman. Lydia thought they must call him that because of the smooth gray overcoat he wore, and his hair, a bright gray which had obviously once been blond. He was not thin or angular and he did not look as if he would be creaky in the joints. He was supple and well-fleshed and dignified and pleasant; fair-skinned, freshly groomed, glistening.

She never told him about that name. She never told him that she had seen him in the bookstore. A week or so later she met him at a publisher's party. He did not remember ever seeing her before, and she supposed he had not seen her, being occupied with chatting with Shirley,

Lydia trusts what she can make of things, usually. She trusts what she thinks about her friend Warren, or his friend

Shirley, and about chance acquaintances, like the couple who run the guesthouse, and Mr. Stanley, and the men she has been playing cards with. She thinks she knows why people behave as they do, and she puts more stock than she will admit in her own unproven theories and unjustified suspicions. But she is stupid and helpless when contemplating the collision of herself and Duncan. She has plenty to say about it, given the chance, because explanation is her habit, but she doesn't trust what she says, even to herself; it doesn't help her. She might just as well cover her head and sit wailing on the ground.

She asks herself what gave him his power. She knows who did. But she asks what, and when—when did the transfer take place, when was the abdication of all pride and sense?

She read for half an hour after getting into bed. Then she went down the hall to the bathroom. It was after midnight. The rest of the house was in darkness. She had left her door ajar, and coming back to her room, she did not turn on the hall light. The door of Eugene's room was also ajar, and as she was passing she heard a low, careful sound. It was like a moan, and also like a whisper. She remembered Lawrence saying Eugene hollered in his sleep, but this sound was not being made in sleep. She knew he was awake. He was watching from the bed in his dark room and he was inviting her. The invitation was amorous and direct and helpless-sounding as his confession of fear when he stood by the window. She went on into her own room and shut the door and hooked it. Even as she did this, she knew she didn't have to. He would never try to get in; there was no bullying spirit in him.

Then she lay awake. Things had changed for her; she refused adventures. She could have gone to Eugene, and earlier in the evening she could have given a sign to Lawrence. In the past she might have done it. She might, or she might not have done it, depending on how she felt. Now it seemed not possible. She felt as if she were muffled up, wrapped in layers and layers of dull knowledge, well protected. It wasn't altogether a bad thing—it left your mind unclouded. Speculation can be more gentle, can take its time, when it is not driven by desire.

She thought about what those men would have been like as lovers. It was Lawrence who would have been her reasonable choice. He was nearest to her own age, and predictable, and probably well used to the discreet encounter. His approach was vulgar, but that would not necessarily have put her off. He would be cheerful, hearty, prudent, perhaps a bit self-congratulatory, attentive in a businesslike way, and he would manage in the middle of his attentions to slip in a warning: a joke, a friendly insult, a reminder of how things stood.

Eugene would never feel the need to do that, though he would have a shorter memory even than Lawrence (much shorter, for Lawrence, though not turning down opportunities, would carry afterward the thought of some bad consequence, for which he must keep ready a sharp line of defense). Eugene would be no less experienced than Lawrence; for years, girls and women must have been answering the kind of plea Lydia had heard, the artless confession. Eugene would be generous, she thought. He would be a grateful, self-forgetful lover, showing his women such kindness that when he left they would never make trouble. They would not try to trap him; they wouldn't whine after him. Women do that to the men who have held back, who have contradicted themselves, promised, lied, mocked. These are the men women get pregnant by, send desperate letters to, preach their own superior love to, take their revenge on. Eugene would go free, he would be an innocent, happy prodigy of love, until he decided it was time to get married. Then he would marry a rather plain, maternal sort of girl, perhaps a bit older than himself, a bit shrewder. He would be faithful, and good to her, and she would manage things; they would raise a large Catholic family.

What about Vincent? Lydia could not imagine him as she easily imagined the others: their noises and movements and bare shoulders and pleasing warm skin; their power, their exertions, their moments of helplessness. She was shy of thinking any such things about him. Yet he was the only one whom she could think of now with real interest. She thought of his courtesy and reticence and humor, his inability to better his luck. She liked him for the very things that made him different from Lawrence and insured that all his life he would be working for Lawrence—or for somebody like Lawrence—never the other way round. She liked him also for the things that made him different from Eugene: the irony, the patience, the self-containment. He was the sort of man she had known when she was a child living on a farm not so different from his, the sort of man who must have been in her family for hundreds of years. She knew his life. With him she could foresee doors opening to what she knew and had forgotten; rooms and landscapes opening; *there*. The rainy evenings, a country with creeks and graveyards, and chokecherry and finches in the fence-corners. She had to wonder if this was what happened, after the years of appetite and greed—did you drift back into tenderhearted fantasies? Or was it just the truth about what she needed and wanted; should she have fallen in love with, and married, a man like Vincent years ago; should she have concentrated on the part of her that would have been content with such an arrange-ment, and forgotten about the rest?

That is, should she have stayed in the place where love is managed for you, not gone where you have to invent it, and reinvent it, and never know if these efforts will be enough?

Duncan spoke about his former girlfriends. Efficient Ruth,

pert Judy, vivacious Diane, elegant Dolores, wifely Maxine. Lorraine the golden-haired, full-breasted beauty; Marian the multilingual; Caroline the neurotic; Rosalie who was wild and gypsylike; gifted, melancholy Louise; serene socialite Jane. What description would do now for Lydia? Lydia the poet. Morose, messy, unsatisfactory Lydia. The unsatisfactory poet.

One Sunday, when they were driving in the hills around Peterborough, he talked about the effects of Lorraine's beauty. Perhaps the voluptuous countryside reminded him. It was almost like a joke, he said. It was almost silly. He stopped for gas in a little town and Lydia went across the street to a discount store that was open Sundays. She bought makeup in tubes off a rack. In the cold and dirty toilet of the gas station she attempted a transformation, slapping buff-colored liquid over her face and rubbing green paste on her eyelids.

"What have you done to your face?" he said when she came back to the car.

"Makeup. I put some makeup on so I'd look more cheerful."

"You can see where the line stops, on your neck."

At such times she felt strangled. It was frustration, she said to the doctor later. The gap between what she wanted and what she could get. She believed that Duncan's love—love for her—was somewhere inside him, and that by gigantic efforts to please, or fits of distress which obliterated all those efforts, or tricks of indifference, she could claw or lure it out.

What gave her such an idea? He did. At least he indicated that he could love her, that they could be happy, if she could honor his privacy, make no demands upon him, and try to alter those things about her person and behavior which he did not like. He listed these things precisely. Some were very intimate in nature and she howled with shame and covered her ears and begged him to take them back or to say no more.

"There is no way to have a discussion with you," he said. He said he hated hysterics, emotional displays, beyond anything, yet she thought she saw a quiver of satisfaction, a deep thrill of relief, that ran through him when she finally broke under the weight of his calm and detailed objections.

"Could that be?" she said to the doctor. "Could it be that he wants a woman close but is so frightened of it he has to try to wreck her? Is that oversimplified?" she said anxiously.

"What about you?" said the doctor. "What do you want?"

"For him to love me?"

"Not for you to love him?"

She thought about Duncan's apartment. There were no curtains; he was higher than the surrounding buildings. No attempt had been made to arrange things to make a setting; nothing was in relation to anything else. Various special requirements had been attended to. A certain sculpture was in a corner behind some filing cabinets because he liked to lie on the floor and look at it in shadow. Books were in piles beside the bed, which was crossways in the room in order to catch the breeze from the window. All disorder was actually order, carefully thought out and not to be interfered with. There was a beautiful little rug at the end of the hall, where he sat and listened to music. There was one great, ugly armchair, a masterpiece of engineering, with all its attachments for the head and limbs. Lydia asked about his guests—how were they accommodated? He replied that he did not have any. The apartment was for himself. He was a popular guest, witty and personable, but not a host, and this seemed reasonable to him, since social life was other people's requirement and invention.

Lydia brought flowers, and there was nowhere to put them except in a jar on the floor by the bed. She brought presents from her trips to Toronto: records, books, cheese. She learned pathways around the apartment and found places where she could sit. She discouraged old friends, or any friends, from phoning or coming to see her, because there was too much she couldn't explain. They saw Duncan's friends sometimes, and she was nervous with them, thinking they were adding her to a list, speculating. She didn't like to see how much he gave them of that store of presents—anecdotes, parodies, flattering wit—which were also used to delight her. He could not bear dullness. She felt that he despised people who were not witty. You needed to be quick to keep up with him in conversation, you needed energy. Lydia saw herself as a dancer on her toes, trembling delicately all over, afraid of letting him down on the next turn.

"Do you mean you think I don't love him?" she said to the doctor.

"How do you know you do?"

"Because I suffer so when he's fed up with me. I want to be wiped off the earth. It's true. I want to hide. I go out on the streets and every face I look at seems to despise me for my failure."

"Your failure to make him love you."

Now Lydia must accuse herself. Her self-absorption equals Duncan's, but is more artfully concealed. She is in competition with him as to who can love best. She is in competition with all other women, even when it is ludicrous for her to be so. She cannot stand to hear them praised or know they are well remembered. Like many women of her generation, she has an idea of love which is ruinous but not serious in some way, not respectful. She is greedy. She talks intelligently and ironically and in this way covers up her indefensible expectations. The sacrifices she made with Duncan—in living arrangements, in the matter of friends, as well as in the rhythm of sex and the tone of conversations— were violations, committed not seriously but flagrantly. That is what was not respectful, that was what was indecent. She made him a present of such power, then complained relentlessly to herself and finally to him, that he had got it. She was out to defeat him.

That is what she says to the doctor. But is it the truth?

"The worst thing is not knowing what is true about any of this. I spend all my waking hours trying to figure out about him and me and I get nowhere. I make wishes. I even pray. I throw money into those wishing wells. I think that there's something in him that's an absolute holdout. There's something in him that has to get rid of me, so he'll find reasons. But he says that's rubbish, he says if I could stop overreacting we'd be happy. I have to think maybe he's right, maybe it is all me."

"When are you happy?"

"When he's pleased with me. When he's joking and enjoying himself. No. No. I'm never happy. What I am is relieved, it's as if I'd overcome a challenge, it's more triumphant than happy. But he can always pull the rug out."

"So, why are you with somebody who can always pull the rug out?"

"Isn't there always somebody? When I was married it was me. Do you think it helps to ask these questions? Suppose it's just pride? I don't want to be alone, I want everybody to think I've got such a desirable man? Suppose it's the humiliation, I want to be humiliated? What good will it do me to know that?"

"I don't know. What do you think?"

"I think these conversations are fine when you're mildly troubled and interested but not when you're desperate."

"You're desperate?"

She felt suddenly tired, almost too tired to speak. The room where she and the doctor were talking had a dark-blue carpet, blue-and-green-striped upholstery. There was a picture of boats and fishermen on the wall. Collusion somewhere, Lydia felt. Fake reassurance, provisional comfort, earnest deceptions.

"No."

It seemed to her that she and Duncan were monsters with a lot of heads, in those days. Out of the mouth of one head could come insult and accusation, hot and cold, out of another false apologies and slimy pleas, out of another just such mealy, reasonable, true-and-false chat as she had practiced with the doctor. Not a mouth would open that had a useful thing to say, not a mouth would have the sense to shut up. At the same time she believed—though she didn't know she believed it—that these monster heads with their cruel and silly and wasteful talk could all be drawn in again, could curl up and go to sleep. Never mind what they'd said; never mind. Then she and Duncan with hope and trust and blank memories could reintroduce themselves, they could pick up the undamaged delight with which they'd started, before they began to put each other to other uses.

When she had been in Toronto a day she tried to retrieve Duncan, by phone, and found that he had acted quickly. He had changed to an unlisted number. He wrote to her, in care of her employer, that he would pack and send her things.

• • •

Lydia had breakfast with Mr. Stanley. The telephone crew had eaten and gone off to work before daylight.

She asked Mr. Stanley about his visit with the woman who had known Willa Cather.

"Ah," said Mr. Stanley, and wiped a corner of his mouth after a bite of poached egg. "She was a woman who used to run a little restaurant down by the dock. She was a good cook, she said. She must have been, because Willa and Edith used to get their dinners from her. She would send it up with her brother, in his car. But sometimes Willa would not be pleased with the dinner—perhaps it would not be quite what she wanted, or she would think it was not cooked as well as it might be—and she would send it back. She would ask for another dinner to be sent." He smiled, and said in a confidential way, "Willa could be imperious. Oh, yes. She was not perfect. All people of great abilities are apt to be impatient in daily matters."

Rubbish, Lydia wanted to say, she sounds a proper bitch.

Sometimes waking up was all right, and sometimes it was very bad. This morning she had wakened with the cold conviction of a mistake—something avoidable and irreparable.

"But sometimes she and Edith would come down to the café," Mr. Stanley continued. "If they felt they wanted some company, they would have dinner there. On one of these occasions Willa had a long talk with the woman I was visiting.

They talked for over an hour. The woman was considering marriage. She had to consider whether to make a marriage that she gave me to understand was something of a business proposition. Companionship. There was no question of romance, she and the gentleman were not young and foolish. Willa talked to her for over an hour. Of course she did not advise her directly to do one thing or the other, she talked to her in general terms very sensibly and kindly and the woman still remembers it vividly. I was happy to hear that but I was not surprised."

"What would she know about it, anyway?" Lydia said.

Mr. Stanley lifted his eyes from his plate and looked at her in grieved amazement.

"Willa Cather lived with a woman," Lydia said.

When Mr. Stanley answered he sounded flustered, and mildly upbraiding.

"They were devoted," he said.

"She never lived with a man."

"She knew things as an artist knows them. Not necessarily by experience."

"But what if they don't know them?" Lydia persisted. "What if they don't?"

He went back to eating his egg as if he had not heard that. Finally he said, "The woman considered Willa's conversation was very helpful to her."

Lydia made a sound of doubtful assent. She knew she

had been rude, even cruel. She knew she would have to apologize. She went to the sideboard and poured herself another cup of coffee.

The woman of the house came in from the kitchen.

"Is it keeping hot? I think I'll have a cup too. Are you really going today? Sometimes I think I'd like to get on a boat and go too. It's lovely here and I love it but you know how you get."

They drank their coffee standing by the sideboard. Lydia did not want to go back to the table, but knew that she would have to. Mr. Stanley looked frail and solitary, with his narrow shoulders, his neat bald head, his brown checked sports jacket which was slightly too large. He took the trouble to be clean and tidy, and it must have been a trouble, with his eyesight. Of all people he did not deserve rudeness.

"Oh, I forgot," the woman said.

She went into the kitchen and came back with a large brown-paper bag.

"Vincent left you this. He said you liked it. Do you?"

Lydia opened the bag and saw long, dark, ragged leaves of dulse, oily-looking even when dry.

"Well," she said.

The woman laughed. "I know. You have to be born here to have the taste."

"No, I do like it," said Lydia. "I was getting to like it."

"You must have made a hit."

Lydia took the bag back to the table and showed it to Mr. Stanley. She tried a conciliatory joke.

"I wonder if Willa Cather ever ate dulse?"

"Dulse," said Mr. Stanley thoughtfully. He reached into the bag and pulled out some leaves and looked at them. Lydia knew he was seeing what Willa Cather might have seen. "She would most certainly have known about it. She would have known."

But was she lucky or was she not, and was it all right with that woman? How did she live? That was what Lydia wanted to say. Would Mr. Stanley have known what she was talking about? If she had asked how did Willa Cather live, would he not have replied that she did not have to find a way to live, as other people did, that she was Willa Cather?

What a lovely, durable shelter he had made for himself. He could carry it everywhere and nobody could interfere with it. The day may come when Lydia will count herself lucky to do the same. In the meantime, she'll be up and down. "Up and down," they used to say in her childhood, talking of the health of people who weren't going to recover. "Ah. She's up and down."

Yet look how this present slyly warmed her, from a distance.

from

HÔTEL DU LAC

ANITA BROOKNER

*Romance novelist Edith Hope has been sent away to the
Hôtel du Lac by her friends, who feel she needs to "come
back older, wiser, and properly apologetic." Her trans-
gression? Jilting a man at the altar, in part because of
her relationship with another who is no nearer to
leaving his wife than he ever was. But at the Hôtel,
Edith meets Philip Neville, who rudely presents
her with an irresistibly hard-hearted
antidote to her heartache.*

'*One hardly notices* the proximity of the glaciers,' said Edith appreciatively.

'No,' agreed Mr Neville. 'But then they are not all that close.'

They were seated outside a small restaurant under a vine-covered trellis, a bottle of yellow wine on the table between them. Shaded, they were able to look out across a small deserted square made brilliant by the sun of early afternoon. At this height the lake mists were no longer imaginable: half-tones and ambiguous gradations, gentle appreciations of mildness and warmth, were banished, relegated to invalid status, by the uncompromising clarity of this higher air. Up here the weather was both hot and cold, bright and dark: hot in the sun, cold in the shade, bright as they climbed, and dark as they had sat in the small deserted café-bar, resting, until Mr Neville had asked, 'Could you walk a little more?' and they had set off again until they reached the top of what seemed to Edith to be a mountain, although the golden fruit on the trees in the terraced orchards they had passed on their way rather gave the lie to this assumption. Now they sat after lunch, becalmed, the only two people contemplating these few square metres of flat cobbled ground, the only sounds the faint whine of a distant car and a mumble of music from a wireless deep in the recesses of the restaurant, perhaps from the kitchen, perhaps from the little sitting room at the back, where the owner might retire to read his newspaper before opening up again for dinner.

But who came here? In Edith's mind, Mrs Pusey and Monica and Mme de Bonneuil, the hotel itself with its elderly pianist and its dependable meals, seemed to be at the other end of the universe. The mild and careful creature that she had been on the lake shore had also disappeared, had dematerialized in the ascent to this upper air, and by a remote and almost crystalline process new components had formed, resulting in something harder, brighter, more decisive, realistic, able to savour enjoyment, even to expect it.

'Who comes here?' she asked.

'People like us,' he replied.

He was a man of few words, but those few words were judiciously selected, weighed for quality, and delivered with expertise. Edith, used to the ruminative monologues that most people consider to be adequate for the purposes of rational discourse, used, moreover, to concocting the cunning and even learned periods which the characters in her books so spontaneously uttered, leaned back in her chair and smiled. The sensation of being entertained by words was one which she encountered all too rarely. People expect writers to entertain *them*, she reflected. They consider that writers should be gratified simply by performing their task to the audience's satisfaction. Like sycophants at court in the

Middle Ages, dwarves, *jongleurs*. And what about us? Nobody thinks about entertaining *us*.

Mr Neville noticed the brief spasm of feeling that passed over Edith's face, and observed, 'You may feel better if you tell me about it.'

'Oh, do you think that is true?' she enquired, breathing rather hard. 'And even if it is, do you guarantee that the results will be immediately felt? Like those obscure advertisements for ointment that help you to "obtain relief." One is never quite sure from what,' she went on. 'Although there is sometimes a tiny drawing of a man, rather correctly dressed, with a hand pressed to the small of his back.'

Mr Neville smiled.

'I suppose it is the promise that counts,' Edith went on, a little wildly. 'Or perhaps just the offer. Anyway, I forget what I was talking about. You mustn't take any notice,' she added. 'Most of my life seems to go on at a subterranean level. And it is too nice a day to bother about all that,' Her face cleared. 'And I am having such a good time,' she said.

She did indeed look as if she might be, he thought. Her face had lost its habitual faintly sheep-like expression, its quest for approval or understanding, and had become amused, patrician. What on earth was she doing here, he wondered.

'What on earth are you doing here?' asked Edith.

He smiled again. 'Why shouldn't I be here?'

She gestured with upturned hands. 'Well, that hotel is hardly the place for you. It seems to be permanently reserved for women. And for a certain kind of woman. Cast-off or abandoned, paid to stay away, or to do harmless womanly things, like spending money on clothes. The very tenor of the conversation excludes men. You must be bored stiff.'

'You, I expect, have come here to finish a book,' he said pleasantly.

Her face clouded. 'That is quite right,' she said. And poured herself another glass of wine.

He affected not to notice this. 'Well, I am rather fond of the place. I came here once with my wife. And as I was at the conference in Geneva, and in no rush to get back, I thought I'd see if it were still the same. The weather was good, so I stayed on a little.'

'This conference,' she said. 'Forgive me, but I don't know what it was about.'

'Electronics. I have a rather sizeable electronics firm which is doing surprisingly well. In fact, it almost runs itself, thanks to my excellent second in command. I spend less and less time there, although I remain responsible for everything that goes on. But this way I can spend a good deal of time on my farm, and that is what I really prefer to do.'

'Where . . . ?'

'Near Marlborough.'

'And your wife,' she ventured. 'Did she not come with you?'

He adjusted the cuffs of his shirt. 'My wife left me three years ago,' he said. 'She ran away with a man ten years her junior, and despite everyone's predictions she is still radiantly happy.'

'Happy,' said Edith lingeringly. 'How marvellous! Oh, I'm so sorry. That was a tactless thing to say. You must think me very stupid.' She sighed. 'I am rather stupid, I fear. Out of phase with the world. People divide writers into two categories,' she went on, deeply embarrassed by his silence. 'Those who are preternaturally wise, and those who are preternaturally naive, as if they had no real experience to go on. I belong in the latter category,' she added, flushing at the truth of what she said. 'Like the Wild Boy of the Aveyron.' Her voice trailed away.

'Now you are looking unhappy,' he observed, after a short silence, during which he allowed her flush to deepen.

'Well, I think I am rather unhappy,' she said. 'And it does so disappoint me.'

'Do you think a lot about being happy?' he asked.

'I think about it all the time.'

'Then, if I may say so, you are wrong to do so. I dare say you are in love,' he said, punishing her for her earlier carelessness. Suddenly there was an antagonism between them, as he intended, for antagonism blunts despair. Edith raised eyes brilliant with anger, only to meet his implacable profile. He was apparently inspecting a butterfly, which had perched, fluttering, on the rim of one of the boxed geranium plants that marked the restaurant's modest perimeter.

'It is a great mistake,' he resumed, after a pause, 'to confuse happiness with one particular situation, one particular person. Since I freed myself from all that I have discovered the secret of contentment.'

'Pray tell me what it is,' she said, in a dry tone. 'I have always wanted to know.'

'It is simply this. Without a huge emotional investment, one can do whatever one pleases. One can take decisions, change one's mind, alter one's plans. There is none of the anxiety of waiting to see if that one other person has everything she desires, if she is discontented, upset, restless, bored. One can be as pleasant or as ruthless as one wants. If one is prepared to do the one thing one is drilled out of doing from earliest childhood—simply please oneself—there is no reason why one should ever be unhappy again.'

'Or, perhaps, entirely happy.'

'Edith, you are a romantic,' he said with a smile. 'I may call you Edith, I hope?'

She nodded. 'But why must I be called a romantic just because I don't see things the same way as you do?'

'Because you are misled by what you would like to believe. Haven't you learned that there is no such thing as complete harmony between two people, however much they profess to love one another? Haven't you realized how much time and

speculation are wasted, how much endless mythological agonizing goes on, simply because they are out of phase? Haven't
you seen how the light touch sometimes, nearly always, in fact,
is more effective than the deepest passion?'

'Yes, I have seen that,' said Edith, sombre.

'Then, my dear, learn to use it. You have no idea how
promising the world begins to look once you have decided to
have it all for yourself. And how much healthier your decisions are once they become entirely selfish. It is the simplest
thing in the world to decide what you want to do—or, rather,
what you don't want to do—and just to act on that.'

'That is true of certain things,' said Edith. 'But not of
others.'

'You must learn to discount the others. Within your own
scope you can accomplish much more. You can be self-
centred, and that is a marvellous lesson to learn. To assume
your own centrality may mean an entirely new life.'

'But if you would prefer to share your life?' asked Edith.
'Supposing that you were a person who was simply bored
with living their own life and wanted to live somebody else's.
For the sheer pleasure of the novelty.'

'You cannot live someone else's life. You can only live
your own. And remember, there are no punishments.
Whatever they told you about unselfishness being good and
wickedness being bad was entirely inaccurate. It is a lesson
for serfs and it leads to resignation. And my policy, you may

be surprised to hear, will ensure you any number of friends. People feel at home with low moral standards. It is scruples that put them off.'

Edith conceded his point with a judicious nod. This dangerous gospel, which she would have refuted at a lower level, seemed to accord with the wine, the brilliance of the sun, the headiness of the air. There was something wrong with it, she knew, but at the moment she was not interested in finding out what it was. More than the force of his argument, she was seduced by the power of his language, his unusual eloquence. And I thought him quiet, she marvelled.

'That is why I so much enjoy our dear Mrs Pusey,' Mr Neville continued. 'There is something quite heartening about her simple greed. And one is so happy to know that she has found the means of satisfying it. And, as you see, she is in good health and spirits: altruism has not interfered with her digestion, conscience has not stopped her sleeping at nights, and she enjoys every minute of her existence.'

'Yes, but I doubt if all this is good for Jennifer,' said Edith. 'Or good enough, I should say. At her age there should be more to life than buying clothes.'

'Jennifer,' said Mr Neville, with his fine smile. 'I have no doubt that in her own way Jennifer is a chip off the old block.'

She leaned back in her chair and raised her face to the sun, mildly intoxicated, not so much by the wine as by the scope of this important argument. Seduced, also, by the possibility that she might please herself, simply by wishing it so. As a devil's advocate Mr Neville was faultless. And yet, she knew, there was a flaw in his reasoning, just as there was a flaw in his ability to feel. Sitting up straight, she returned to the attack.

'This life you advocate,' she queried, 'with its low moral standards. Can you recommend it? For others, I mean.'

Mr Neville's smile deepened. 'I daresay my wife could. And that is what you are getting at, isn't it? Do I tolerate low moral standards in other people?'

Edith nodded.

He took a sip of his wine.

'I have come to understand them very well,' he replied.

Well done, thought Edith. That was a faultless performance. He knew what I was thinking and he gave me an answer. Not a satisfactory answer, but an honest one. And in its own way, elegant. I suppose Mr Neville is what was once called a man of quality. He conducts himself altogether gracefully. He is well turned out, she thought, surveying the panama hat and the linen jacket. He is even good-looking: an eighteenth-century face, fine, reticent, full-lipped, with a faint bluish gleam of beard just visible beneath the healthy skin. A heartless man, I think. Furiously intelligent. Suitable. Oh David, David.

Mr Neville, noting the minute alteration in her attention to him, leaned over the table.

'You are wrong to think that you cannot live without love, Edith.'

'No, I am not wrong,' she said, slowly. 'I cannot live without it. Oh, I do not mean that I go into a decline, develop odd symptoms, become a caricature. I mean something far more serious than that. I mean that I cannot live *well* without it. I cannot think or act or speak or write or even dream with any kind of energy in the absence of love. I feel excluded from the living world. I become cold, fish-like, immobile. I implode. My idea of absolute happiness is to sit in a hot garden all day, reading, or writing, utterly safe in the knowledge that the person I love will come home to me in the evening. Every evening.'

'You are a romantic, Edith,' repeated Mr Neville, with a smile.

'It is you who are wrong,' she replied. 'I have been listening to that particular accusation for most of my life. I am not a romantic. I am a domestic animal. I do not sigh and yearn for extravagant displays of passion, for the grand affair, the world well lost for love. I know all that, and know that it leaves you lonely. No, what I crave is the simplicity of routine. An evening walk, arm in arm, in fine weather. A game of cards. Time for idle talk. Preparing a meal together.'

'Putting the cat out?' suggested Mr Neville.

Edith gave him a glance of pure dislike.

'That's better,' he said.

'Well, you obviously find this very amusing,' she said. 'Clearly they order things better in Swindon, or wherever it was that you . . . I'm sorry. I shouldn't have said that. It was extremely rude of me. How dreadfully . . .'.

He poured her out another glass of wine.

'You are a good woman,' he said. 'That is all too obvious.'

'How is it obvious?' she asked.

'Good women always think it is their fault when someone else is being offensive. Bad women never take the blame for anything.'

Edith, breathing hard, wondered if she were drunk or simply rendered incautious by the novelty of this conversation.

'I should like some coffee,' she announced, with what she hoped was Nietzschean directness. 'No, on second thoughts, I should like some tea. I should like a pot of very strong tea.'

Mr Neville glanced at his watch. 'Yes,' he said. 'It is getting on. We should be making a move soon. When you have had your tea,' he added.

Edith drank her tea fiercely, unaware that the exertion of thinking, so remote, so unusual in her present circumstances, had brought colour to her cheeks and added brightness to her eyes. Her hair, slipping from its usual tight control, lay untidily on her neck, and with a gesture of impatience she removed the last securing hairpins, raked her fingers through it, and let it fall about her face. Mr Neville, appraising her with faintly pursed lips, nodded.

'Let me tell you what you need, Edith,' he said.

Not again, she thought. I have just told you what I need and I know what that is better than you do.

'Yes, I know you think you know better than I do,' he said, as her head shot up in alarm. 'But you are wrong. You do not need more love. You need less. Love has not done you much good, Edith. Love has made you secretive, self-effacing, perhaps dishonest?'

She nodded.

'Love has brought you to the Hotel du Lac, out of season, to sit with the other women, and talk about clothes. Is that what you want?'

'No,' she said. 'No.'

'No,' he went on. 'You are a clever woman, too clever not to know what you are missing. Those tiny domestic pleasures, those card games you talk about, they would soon pall.'

'No,' she repeated. 'Never.'

'Yes. Oh, your romanticism might keep rueful thoughts at bay for a time, but the thoughts would win out. And then you would discover that you had a lot in common with all the other discontented women, and you'd start to see a lot of sense in the feminist position, and you'd refuse to read anything but women's novels . . .'

'I write them,' she reminded him.

'Not that sort,' he said. 'You write about love. And you

will never write anything different, I suspect, until you begin to take a harder look at yourself.'

Edith felt the hairs on the back of her neck begin to crepitate. She had told herself as much, many times, but had been able to dismiss her own verdict. Now she recognized the voice of authority, as if she had heard an illness confirmed, although she had almost succeeded in persuading herself that she was only imagining the symptoms.

'Do you really want to spend the rest of your life talking to aggrieved women about your womb?' he went on, inexorably.

'I really don't think I have much of a womb to talk about,' she said, with an unhappy laugh.

'Oh, you would become gloomy about it in due course. In any event, I doubt if anyone's bears close inspection.'

'Tell me,' said Edith, after a pause, 'you don't by any chance do psychiatry as a sideline, do you? Since the electronics industry leaves you so much spare time?'

'What you need, Edith, is not love. What you need is a social position. What you need is marriage.'

'I know,' she said.

'And once you are married, you can behave as badly as everybody else. Worse, given your unused capacity.'

'The relief,' she agreed.

'And you will be popular with one and all, and have so much more to talk about. And never have to wait by the telephone again.'

Edith stood up. 'It's getting cold,' she said. 'Shall we go?'

She strode on ahead of him. That last remark was regrettable, she thought. Vulgar. And he knows where to plant the knife. Yes, writing in my room leaves me free to be telephoned; who knows what might happen if I went out? And suddenly she longed for such solitude, like a child who has become overexcited at a party, and who should have been taken home, by a prudent nurse, some time ago.

'I am sorry,' he said, catching her up. 'Please. I don't want to pry. I know nothing about you. You are an excellent woman, and I have offended you. Please forgive me.'

'You are sadistic,' she said, pleasantly.

He inclined his head. 'So my wife used to tell me.'

'And how do you know that my capacity for bad behaviour is unused? That is a mild but definite form of sexual insult, you know. Less well publicized than bottom-pinching or harassment at work, but one with which quite a lot of women are familiar.'

'If your capacity for bad behaviour were being properly used, you would not be moping around in that cardigan.'

Edith shot ahead, furious. To contain her anger—for she could not find her way down to the lake unaided—she tried various distancing procedures, familiar to her from long use. The most productive was to convert the incident into a scene in one of her novels. 'The evening came on stealthily,' she muttered to herself. 'The sun, a glowing ball . . .'. It was no good. She turned round, searching for him, listening for the steps which should be following her and were not, and feeling suddenly alone on this hillside, in the cold. She shivered and wrapped her arms around herself.

'I hate you,' she shouted, hopefully.

A steady crunch of gravel announced the reappearance of Mr Neville. When his face came into focus, Edith saw that it was wearing its usual smile, intensified.

'You are coming along very well,' he said, taking her arm.

'You know,' she said, after ten minutes of silent descent. 'I find that smile of yours just the faintest bit unamiable.'

His smile broadened. 'When you get to know me better,' he remarked, 'you will realize just how unamiable it really is.'

THE BRIDAL PARTY

F. SCOTT FITZGERALD

First love, tinged with youth, wonder, and discovery,
is probably the hardest to forget. Michael Curly has
tried to forget by moving to Paris while his lost
Caroline remains in New York. When Caroline
comes to France to be married, Michael
finds that distance wasn't the
answer after all.

There was the usual insincere little note saying: "I wanted you to be the first to know." It was a double shock to Michael, announcing, as it did, both the engagement and the imminent marriage; which, moreover, was to be held, not in New York, decently and far away, but here in Paris under his very nose, if that could be said to extend over the Protestant Episcopal Church of the Holy Trinity, Avenue George-Cinq. The date was two weeks off, early in June.

At first Michael was afraid and his stomach felt hollow. When he left the hotel that morning, the *femme de chambre*, who was in love with his fine, sharp profile and his pleasant buoyancy, scented the hard abstraction that had settled over him. He walked in a daze to his bank, he bought a detective story at Smith's on the Rue de Rivoli, he sympathetically stared for a while at a faded panorama of the battlefields in a tourist-office window and cursed a Greek tout who followed him with a half-displayed packet of innocuous postcards warranted to be very dirty indeed.

But the fear stayed with him, and after a while he recognized it as the fear that now he would never be happy. He had met Caroline Dandy when she was seventeen, possessed her young heart all through her first season in New York, and then lost her, slowly, tragically, uselessly, because he had no money and could make no money; because, with all the energy and good will in the world, he could not find himself; because, loving him still, Caroline had lost faith and begun to see him as something pathetic, futile and shabby, outside the great, shining stream of life toward which she was inevitably drawn.

Since his only support was that she loved him, he leaned weakly on that; the support broke, but still he held on to it and was carried out to sea and washed up on the French coast with its broken pieces still in his hands. He carried them around with him in the form of photographs and packets of correspondence and a liking for a maudlin popular song called "Among My Souvenirs." He kept clear of other girls, as if Caroline would somehow know it and reciprocate with a faithful heart. Her note informed him that he had lost her forever.

It was a fine morning. In front of the shops in the Rue de Castiglione, proprietors and patrons were on the sidewalk gazing upward, for the Graf Zeppelin, shining and glorious, symbol of escape and destruction—of escape, if necessary, through destruction—glided in the Paris sky. He heard a woman say in French that it would not astonish her if that commenced to let fall the bombs. Then he heard another voice, full of husky laughter, and the void in his stomach froze. Jerking about, he was face to face with Caroline Dandy and her fiancé.

"Why, Michael! Why, we were wondering where you

were. I asked at the Guaranty Trust, and the Morgan and Company, and finally sent a note to the National City—"

Why didn't they back away? Why didn't they back right up, walking backward down the Rue de Castiglione, across the Rue de Rivoli, through the Tuileries Gardens, still walking backward as fast as they could till they grew vague and faded out across the river?

"This is Hamilton Rutherford, my fiancé."

"We've met before."

"At Pat's, wasn't it?"

"And last spring in the Ritz Bar."

"Michael, where have you been keeping yourself?"

"Around here." This agony. Previews of Hamilton Rutherford flashed before his eyes—a quick series of pictures, sentences. He remembered hearing that he had bought a seat in 1920 for a hundred and twenty-five thousand of borrowed money, and just before the break sold it for more than half a million. Not handsome like Michael, but vitally attractive, confident, authoritative, just the right height over Caroline there—Michael had always been too short for Caroline when they danced.

Rutherford was saying: "No, I'd like it very much if you'd come to the bachelor dinner. I'm taking the Ritz Bar from nine o'clock on. Then right after the wedding there'll be a reception and breakfast at the Hotel George-Cinq."

"And, Michael, George Packman is giving a party day

after tomorrow at Chez Victor, and I want you to be sure and come. And also to tea Friday at Jebby West's; she'd want to have you if she knew where you were. What's your hotel, so we can send you an invitation? You see, the reason we decided to have it over here is because mother has been sick in a nursing home here and the whole clan is in Paris. Then Hamilton's mother's being here too—"

The entire clan; they had always hated him, except her mother; always discouraged his courtship. What a little counter he was in this game of families and money! Under his hat his brow sweated with the humiliation of the fact that for all his misery he was worth just exactly so many invitations. Frantically he began to mumble something about going away.

Then it happened—Caroline saw deep into him, and Michael knew that she saw. She saw through to his profound woundedness, and something quivered inside her, died out along the curve of her mouth and in her eyes. He had moved her. All the unforgettable impulses of first love had surged up once more; their hearts had in some way touched across two feet of Paris sunlight. She took her fiancé's arm suddenly, as if to steady herself with the feel of it.

They parted. Michael walked quickly for a minute; then he stopped, pretending to look in a window, and saw them farther up the street, walking fast into the Place Vendôme, people with much to do.

He had things to do also—he had to get his laundry.

"Nothing will ever be the same again," he said to himself. "She will never be happy in her marriage and I will never be happy at all anymore."

The two vivid years of his love for Caroline moved back around him like years in Einstein's physics. Intolerable memories arose—of rides in the Long Island moonlight; of a happy time at Lake Placid with her cheeks so cold there, but warm just underneath the surface; of a despairing afternoon in a little café on Forty-eighth Street in the last sad months when their marriage had come to seem impossible.

"Come in," he said aloud.

The concierge with a telegram; brusque because Mr. Curly's clothes were a little shabby. Mr. Curly gave few tips; Mr. Curly was obviously a *petit client*.

Michael read the telegram.

"An answer?" the concierge asked.

"No," said Michael, and then, on an impulse: "Look."

"Too bad—too bad," said the concierge. "Your grandfather is dead."

"Not too bad," said Michael. "It means that I come into a quarter of a million dollars."

Too late by a single month; after the first flush of the news his misery was deeper than ever. Lying awake in bed that night, he listened endlessly to the caravan of a circus moving through the street from one Paris fair to another.

When the last van had rumbled out of hearing and the

corners of the furniture were pastel blue with the dawn, he was still thinking of the look in Caroline's eyes that morning—the look that seemed to say: "Oh, why couldn't you have done something about it? Why couldn't you have been stronger, made me marry you? Don't you see how sad I am?"

Michael's fists clenched.

"Well, I won't give up till the last moment," he whispered. "I've had all the bad luck so far, and maybe it's turned at last. One takes what one can get, up to the limit of one's strength, and if I can't have her, at least she'll go into this marriage with some of me in her heart."

II.

Accordingly he went to the party at Chez Victor two days later, upstairs and into the little salon off the bar where the party was to assemble for cocktails. He was early; the only other occupant was a tall lean man of fifty. They spoke.

"You waiting for George Packman's party?"

"Yes. My name's Michael Curly."

"My name's—"

Michael failed to catch the name. They ordered a drink, and Michael supposed that the bride and groom were having a gay time.

"Too much so," the other agreed, frowning. "I don't see how they stand it. We all crossed on the boat together; five days of that crazy life and then two weeks of Paris. You"—he hesitated, smiling faintly—"you'll excuse me for saying that your generation drinks too much."

"Not Caroline."

"No, not Caroline. She seems to take only a cocktail and a glass of champagne, and then she's had enough, thank God. But Hamilton drinks too much and all this crowd of young people drink too much. Do you live in Paris?"

"For the moment," said Michael.

"I don't like Paris. My wife—that is to say, my ex-wife, Hamilton's mother—lives in Paris."

"You're Hamilton Rutherford's father?"

"I have that honor. And I'm not denying that I'm proud of what he's done; it was just a general comment."

"Of course."

Michael glanced up nervously as four people came in. He felt suddenly that his dinner coat was old and shiny; he had ordered a new one that morning. The people who had come in were rich and at home in their richness with one another— a dark, lovely girl with a hysterical little laugh whom he had met before; two confident men whose jokes referred invariably to last night's scandal and tonight's potentialities, as if they had important roles in a play that extended indefinitely into the past and the future. When Caroline arrived, Michael had scarcely a moment of her, but it was enough to note that, like all the others, she was strained and tired. She was pale beneath her rouge; there were shadows under her eyes. With a mixture of relief and wounded vanity, he found himself placed far from her and at another table; he needed a moment to adjust himself to his surroundings. This was not like the immature set in which he and Caroline had moved; the men were more than thirty and had an air of sharing the best of this world's good. Next to him was Jebby West, whom he knew; and, on the other side, a jovial man who immediately began to talk to Michael about a stunt for the bachelor dinner: They were going to hire a French girl to appear with an actual baby in her arms, crying: "Hamilton, you can't desert me now!" The idea seemed stale and unamusing to Michael, but its originator shook with anticipatory laughter.

Farther up the table there was talk of the market—another drop today, the most appreciable since the crash; people were kidding Rutherford about it: "Too bad, old man. You better not get married, after all."

Michael asked the man on his left, "Has he lost a lot?"

"Nobody knows. He's heavily involved, but he's one of the smartest young men in Wall Street. Anyhow, nobody ever tells you the truth."

It was a champagne dinner from the start, and toward the end it reached a pleasant level of conviviality, but Michael saw that all these people were too weary to be exhilarated by any ordinary stimulant; for weeks they had drunk cocktails before meals like Americans, wines and brandies like

Frenchmen, beer like Germans, whiskey-and-soda like the English, and as they were no longer in the twenties, this preposterous *mélange*, that was like some gigantic cocktail in a nightmare, served only to make them temporarily less conscious of the mistakes of the night before. Which is to say that it was not really a gay party; what gayety existed was displayed in the few who drank nothing at all.

But Michael was not tired, and the champagne stimulated him and made his misery less acute. He had been away from New York for more than eight months and most of the dance music was unfamiliar to him, but at the first bars of the "Painted Doll," to which he and Caroline had moved through so much happiness and despair the previous summer, he crossed to Caroline's table and asked her to dance.

She was lovely in a dress of thin ethereal blue, and the proximity of her crackly yellow hair, of her cool and tender gray eyes, turned his body clumsy and rigid; he stumbled with their first step on the floor. For a moment it seemed that there was nothing to say; he wanted to tell her about his inheritance, but the idea seemed abrupt, unprepared for.

"Michael, it's so nice to be dancing with you again."

He smiled grimly.

"I'm so happy you came," she continued. "I was afraid maybe you'd be silly and stay away. Now we can be just good friends and natural together. Michael, I want you and Hamilton to like each other."

The engagement was making her stupid; he had never heard her make such a series of obvious remarks before.

"I could kill him without a qualm," he said pleasantly, "but he looks like a good man. He's fine. What I want to know is, what happens to people like me who aren't able to forget?"

As he said this he could not prevent his mouth from dropping suddenly, and glancing up, Caroline saw, and her heart quivered violently, as it had the other morning.

"Do you mind so much, Michael?"

"Yes."

For a second as he said this, in a voice that seemed to have come up from his shoes, they were not dancing; they were simply clinging together. Then she leaned away from him and twisted her mouth into a lovely smile.

"I didn't know what to do at first, Michael. I told Hamilton about you—that I'd cared for you an awful lot—but it didn't worry him, and he was right. Because I'm over you now—yes, I am. And you'll wake up some sunny morning and be over me just like that."

He shook his head stubbornly.

"Oh, yes. We weren't for each other. I'm pretty flighty, and I need somebody like Hamilton to decide things. It was that more than the question of—of—"

"Of money." Again he was on the point of telling her what had happened, but again something told him it was not the time.

"Then how do you account for what happened when we met the other day," he demanded helplessly—"what happened just now? When we just pour toward each other like we used to—as if we were one person, as if the same blood was flowing through both of us?"

"Oh, don't," she begged him. "You mustn't talk like that; everything's decided now. I love Hamilton with all my heart. It's just that I remember certain things in the past and I feel sorry for you—for us—for the way we were."

Over her shoulder, Michael saw a man come toward them to cut in. In a panic he danced her away, but inevitably the man came on.

"I've got to see you alone, if only for a minute," Michael said quickly. "When can I?"

"I'll be at Jebby West's tea tomorrow," she whispered as a hand fell politely upon Michael's shoulder.

But he did not talk to her at Jebby West's tea. Rutherford stood next to her, and each brought the other into all conversations. They left early. The next morning the wedding cards arrived in the first mail.

Then Michael, grown desperate with pacing up and down his room, determined on a bold stroke; he wrote to Hamilton Rutherford, asking him for a rendezvous the following afternoon. In a short telephone communication Rutherford agreed, but for a day later than Michael had asked. And the wedding was only six days away.

They were to meet in the bar of the Hotel Jena. Michael knew what he would say: "See here, Rutherford, do you realize the responsibility you're taking in going through with this marriage? Do you realize the harvest of trouble and regret you're sowing in persuading a girl into something contrary to the instincts of her heart?" He would explain that the barrier between Caroline and himself had been an artificial one and was now removed, and demand that the matter be put up to Caroline frankly before it was too late.

Rutherford would be angry, conceivably there would be a scene, but Michael felt that he was fighting for his life now.

He found Rutherford in conversation with an older man, whom Michael had met at several of the wedding parties.

"I saw what happened to most of my friends," Rutherford was saying, "and I decided it wasn't going to happen to me. It isn't so difficult; if you take a girl with common sense, and tell her what's what, and do your stuff damn well, and play decently square with her, it's a marriage. If you stand for any nonsense at the beginning, it's one of these arrangements— within five years the man gets out, or else the girl gobbles him up and you have the usual mess."

"Right!" agreed his companion enthusiastically. "Hamilton, boy, you're right."

Michael's blood boiled slowly.

"Doesn't it strike you," he inquired coldly, "that your attitude went out of fashion a hundred years ago?"

"No, it didn't," said Rutherford pleasantly, but impatiently. "I'm as modern as anybody. I'd get married in an aeroplane next Saturday if it'd please my girl."

"I don't mean that way of being modern. You can't take a sensitive woman—"

"Sensitive? Women aren't so darn sensitive. It's fellows like you who are sensitive; it's fellows like you they exploit—all your devotion and kindness and all that. They read a couple of books and see a few pictures because they haven't got anything else to do, and then they say they're finer in grain than you are, and to prove it they take the bit in their teeth and tear off for a fare-you-well—just about as sensitive as a fire horse."

"Caroline happens to be sensitive," said Michael in a clipped voice.

At this point the other man got up to go; when the dispute about the check had been settled and they were alone, Rutherford leaned back to Michael as if a question had been asked him.

"Caroline's more than sensitive," he said. "She's got sense."

His combative eyes, meeting Michael's, flickered with a gray light. "This all sounds pretty crude to you, Mr. Curly, but it seems to me that the average man nowadays just asks to be made a monkey of by some woman who doesn't even get any fun out of reducing him to that level. There are darn few men who possess their wives anymore, but I am going to be one of them."

To Michael it seemed time to bring the talk back to the actual situation: "Do you realize the responsibility you're taking?"

"I certainly do," interrupted Rutherford. "I'm not afraid of responsibility. I'll make the decisions—fairly, I hope, but anyhow they'll be final."

"What if you didn't start right?" said Michael impetuously. "What if your marriage isn't founded on mutual love?"

"I think I see what you mean," Rutherford said, still pleasant. "And since you've brought it up, let me say that if you and Caroline had married, it wouldn't have lasted three years. Do you know what your affair was founded on? On sorrow. You got sorry for each other. Sorrow's a lot of fun for most women and for some men, but it seems to me that a marriage ought to be based on hope." He looked at his watch and stood up.

"I've got to meet Caroline. Remember, you're coming to the bachelor dinner day after tomorrow."

Michael felt the moment slipping away. "Then Caroline's personal feelings don't count with you?" he demanded fiercely.

"Caroline's tired and upset. But she has what she wants, and that's the main thing."

"Are you referring to yourself?" demanded Michael incredulously.

"Yes."

"May I ask how long she's wanted you?"

"About two years." Before Michael could answer, he was gone.

During the next two days Michael floated in an abyss of helplessness. The idea haunted him that he had left something undone that would sever this knot drawn tighter under his eyes. He phoned Caroline, but she insisted that it was physically impossible for her to see him until the day before the wedding, for which day she granted him a tentative rendezvous. Then he went to the bachelor dinner, partly in fear of an evening alone at his hotel, partly from a feeling that by his presence at that function he was somehow nearer to Caroline, keeping her in sight.

The Ritz Bar had been prepared for the occasion by French and American banners and by a great canvas covering one wall, against which the guests were invited to concentrate their proclivities in breaking glasses.

At the first cocktail, taken at the bar, there were many slight spillings from many trembling hands, but later, with the champagne, there was a rising tide of laughter and occasional bursts of song.

Michael was surprised to find what a difference his new dinner coat, his new silk hat, his new, proud linen made in his estimate of himself; he felt less resentment toward all these people for being so rich and assured. For the first time since he had left college he felt rich and assured himself; he felt that he was part of all this, and even entered into the scheme of Johnson, the practical joker, for the appearance of the woman betrayed, now waiting tranquilly in the room across the hall.

"We don't want to go too heavy," Johnson said, "because I imagine Ham's had a pretty anxious day already. Did you see Fullman Oil's sixteen points off this morning?"

"Will that matter to him?" Michael asked, trying to keep the interest out of his voice.

"Naturally. He's in heavily; he's always in everything heavily. So far he's had luck; anyhow, up to a month ago."

The glasses were filled and emptied faster now, and men were shouting at one another across the narrow table. Against the bar a group of ushers was being photographed, and the flash light surged through the room in a stifling cloud.

"Now's the time," Johnson said. "You're to stand by the door, remember, and we're both to try and keep her from coming in—just till we get everybody's attention."

He went on out into the corridor, and Michael waited obediently by the door. Several minutes passed. Then Johnson reappeared with a curious expression on his face.

"There's something funny about this."

"Isn't the girl there?"

"She's there all right, but there's another woman there, too; and it's nobody we engaged either. She wants to see

Hamilton Rutherford, and she looks as if she had something on her mind."

They went out into the hall. Planted firmly in a chair near the door sat an American girl a little worse for liquor, but with a determined expression on her face. She looked up at them with a jerk of her head.

"Well, j'tell him?" she demanded. "The name is Marjorie Collins, and he'll know it. I've come a long way, and I want to see him now and quick, or there's going to be more trouble than you ever saw." She rose unsteadily to her feet.

"You go in and tell Ham," whispered Johnson to Michael. "Maybe he'd better get out. I'll keep her here."

Back at the table, Michael leaned close to Rutherford's ear and, with a certain grimness, whispered:

"A girl outside named Marjorie Collins says she wants to see you. She looks as if she wanted to make trouble."

Hamilton Rutherford blinked and his mouth fell ajar; then slowly the lips came together in a straight line and he said in a crisp voice:

"Please keep her there. And send the head barman to me right away."

Michael spoke to the barman, and then, without returning to the table, asked quietly for his coat and hat. Out in the hall again, he passed Johnson and the girl without speaking and went out into the Rue Cambon. Calling a cab, he gave the address of Caroline's hotel.

His place was beside her now. Not to bring bad news, but simply to be with her when her house of cards came falling around her head.

Rutherford had implied that he was soft—well, he was hard enough not to give up the girl he loved without taking advantage of every chance within the pale of honor. Should she turn away from Rutherford, she would find him there.

She was in; she was surprised when he called, but she was still dressed and would be down immediately. Presently she appeared in a dinner gown, holding two blue telegrams in her hand. They sat down in armchairs in the deserted lobby.

"But, Michael, is the dinner over?"

"I wanted to see you, so I came away."

"I'm glad." Her voice was friendly, but matter-of-fact. "Because I'd just phoned your hotel that I had fittings and rehearsals all day tomorrow. Now we can have our talk after all."

"You're tired," he guessed. "Perhaps I shouldn't have come."

"No. I was waiting for Hamilton. Telegrams that may be important. He said he might go on somewhere, and that may mean any hour, so I'm glad to have someone to talk to."

Michael winced at the impersonality in the last phrase.

"Don't you care when he gets home?"

"Naturally," she said, laughing, "but I haven't got much to say about it, have I?"

"Why not?"

"I couldn't start by telling him what he could and couldn't do."

"Why not?"

"He wouldn't stand for it."

"He seems to want merely a housekeeper," said Michael ironically.

"Tell me about your plans, Michael," she asked quickly.

"My plans? I can't see any future after the day after tomorrow. The only real plan I ever had was to love you."

Their eyes brushed past each other's, and the look he knew so well was staring out at him from hers. Words flowed quickly from his heart:

"Let me tell you just once more how well I've loved you, never wavering for a moment, never thinking of another girl. And now when I think of all the years ahead without you, without any hope, I don't want to live, Caroline darling. I used to dream about our home, our children, about holding you in my arms and touching your face and hands and hair that used to belong to me, and now I just can't wake up."

Caroline was crying softly. "Poor Michael—poor Michael." Her hand reached out and her fingers brushed the lapel of his dinner coat. "I was so sorry for you the other night. You looked so thin, and as if you needed a new suit and somebody to take care of you." She sniffled and looked more closely at his coat. "Why, you've got a new suit! And a new silk hat! Why, Michael, how swell!" She laughed, suddenly cheerful through her tears. "You must have come into money, Michael; I never saw you so well turned out."

For a moment, at her reaction, he hated his new clothes.

"I have come into money," he said. "My grandfather left me about a quarter of a million dollars."

"Why, Michael," she cried, "how perfectly swell! I can't tell you how glad I am. I've always thought you were the sort of person who ought to have money."

"Yes, just too late to make a difference."

The revolving door from the street groaned around and Hamilton Rutherford came into the lobby. His face was flushed, his eyes were restless and impatient.

"Hello, darling; hello, Mr. Curly." He bent and kissed Caroline. "I broke away for a minute to find out if I had any telegrams. I see you've got them there." Taking them from her, he remarked to Curly, "That was an odd business in the bar, wasn't it? Especially as I understand some of you had a joke fixed up in the same line." He opened one of the telegrams, closed it and turned to Caroline with the divided expression of a man carrying two things in his head at once.

"A girl I haven't seen for two years turned up," he said. "It seemed to be some clumsy form of blackmail, for I haven't and never have had any sort of obligation toward her whatever."

"What happened?"

"The head barman had a Sûreté Générale man there in ten minutes and it was settled in the hall. The French blackmail laws make ours look like a sweet wish, and I gather they threw a scare into her that she'll remember. But it seems wiser to tell you."

"Are you implying that I mentioned the matter?" said Michael stiffly.

"No," Rutherford said slowly. "No, you were just going to be on hand. And since you're here, I'll tell you some news that will interest you even more."

He handed Michael one telegram and opened the other.

"This is in code," Michael said.

"So is this. But I've got to know all the words pretty well this last week. The two of them together mean that I'm due to start life all over."

Michael saw Caroline's face grow a shade paler, but she sat quiet as a mouse.

"It was a mistake and I stuck to it too long," continued Rutherford. "So you see I don't have all the luck, Mr. Curly. By the way, they tell me you've come into money."

"Yes," said Michael.

"There we are, then." Rutherford turned to Caroline. "You understand, darling, that I'm not joking or exaggerating. I've lost almost every cent I had and I'm starting life over."

Two pairs of eyes were regarding her—Rutherford's noncommittal and unrequiring, Michael's hungry, tragic, pleading. In a minute she had raised herself from the chair and with a little cry thrown herself into Hamilton Rutherford's arms.

"Oh, darling," she cried, "what does it matter! It's better; I like it better, honestly I do! I want to start that way; I want to! Oh, please don't worry or be sad even for a minute."

"All right, baby," said Rutherford. His hands stroked her hair gently for a moment; then he took his arm from around her.

"I promised to join the party for an hour," he said. "So I'll say good night, and I want you to go to bed soon and get a good sleep. Good night, Mr. Curly. I'm sorry to have let you in for all these financial matters."

But Michael had already picked up his hat and cane. "I'll go along with you," he said.

III.

It was such a fine morning. Michael's cutaway hadn't been delivered, so he felt rather uncomfortable passing before the cameras and moving-picture machines in front of the little church on the Avenue George-Cinq.

It was such a clean, new church that it seemed unforgivable not to be dressed properly, and Michael, white and shaky after a sleepless night, decided to stand in the rear. From there he looked at the back of Hamilton Rutherford, and the lacy, filmy back of Caroline, and the fat back of George Packman, which looked unsteady, as if it wanted to lean against the bride and groom.

The ceremony went on for a long time under gray flags and pennons overhead, under the thick beams of June sunlight slanting down through the tall windows upon the well-dressed people.

As the procession, headed by the bride and groom, started down the aisle, Michael realized with alarm he was just where everyone would dispense with their parade stiffness, become informal and speak to him.

So it turned out. Rutherford and Caroline spoke first to him; Rutherford grim with the strain of being married, and Caroline lovelier than he had ever seen her, floating all softly down through the friends and relatives of her youth, down through the past and forward to the future by the sunlit door.

Michael managed to murmur, "Beautiful, simply beautiful," and then other people passed and spoke to him—old Mrs. Dandy, straight from her sickbed and looking remarkably well, or carrying it off like the very fine old lady she was; and Rutherford's father and mother, ten years divorced, but walking side by side and looking made for each other and proud. Then all Caroline's sisters and their husbands and her little nephews in Eton suits, and then a long parade, all speaking to Michael because he was still standing paralyzed just at that point where the procession broke.

He wondered what would happen now. Cards had been issued for a reception at the George-Cinq; an expensive enough place, heaven knew. Would Rutherford try to go through with that on top of those disastrous telegrams? Evidently, for the procession outside was streaming up there through the June morning, three by three and four by four. On the corner the long dresses of girls, five abreast, fluttered many-colored in the wind. Girls had become gossamer again, perambulatory flora; such lovely fluttering dresses in the bright noon wind.

Michael needed a drink; he couldn't face that reception line without a drink. Diving into a side doorway of the hotel, he asked for the bar, whither a *chasseur* led him through half a kilometer of new American-looking passages.

But—how did it happen?—the bar was full. There were ten—fifteen men and two—four girls, all from the wedding, all needing a drink. There were cocktails and champagne in the bar; Rutherford's cocktails and champagne, as it turned out, for he had engaged the whole bar and the ballroom and the two great reception rooms and all the stairways leading up and down, and windows looking out over the whole square block of Paris. By and by Michael went and joined the long, slow drift of the receiving line. Through a flowery mist of "Such a lovely wedding," "My dear, you were simply lovely," "You're a lucky man, Rutherford" he passed down the line. When Michael came to Caroline, she took a single

step forward and kissed him on the lips, but he felt no contact in the kiss; it was unreal and he floated on away from it.
Old Mrs. Dandy, who had always liked him, held his hand for
a minute and thanked him for the flowers he had sent when
he heard she was ill.

"I'm so sorry not to have written; you know, we old
ladies are grateful for—" The flowers, the fact that she had
not written, the wedding—Michael saw that they all had the
same relative importance to her now; she had married off five
other children and seen two of the marriages go to pieces,
and this scene, so poignant, so confusing to Michael,
appeared to her simply a familiar charade in which she had
played her part before.

A buffet luncheon with champagne was already being
served at small tables and there was an orchestra playing in
an empty ballroom. Michael sat down with Jebby West; he
was still a little embarrassed at not wearing a morning coat,
but he perceived now that he was not alone in the omission
and felt better. "Wasn't Caroline divine?" Jebby West said.
"So entirely self-possessed. I asked her this morning if she
wasn't a little nervous at stepping off like this. And she said,
'Why should I be? I've been after him for two years, and now
I'm just happy, that's all.'"

"It must be true," said Michael gloomily.

"What?"

"What you just said."

He had been stabbed, but, rather to his distress, he did not feel the wound.

He asked Jebby to dance. Out on the floor, Rutherford's father and mother were dancing together.

"It makes me a little sad, that," she said. "Those two hadn't met for years; both of them were married again and she divorced again. She went to the station to meet him when he came over for Caroline's wedding, and invited him to stay at her house in the Avenue du Bois with a whole lot of other people, perfectly proper, but he was afraid his wife would hear about it and not like it, so he went to a hotel. Don't you think that's sort of sad?"

An hour or so later Michael realized suddenly that it was afternoon. In one corner of the ballroom an arrangement of screens like a moving-picture stage had been set up and photographers were taking official pictures of the bridal party. The bridal party, still as death and pale as wax under the bright lights, appeared, to the dancers circling the modulated semidarkness of the ballroom, like those jovial or sinister groups that one comes upon in The Old Mill at an amusement park.

After the bridal party had been photographed, there was a group of the ushers; then the bridesmaids, the families, the children. Later, Caroline, active and excited, having long since abandoned the repose implicit in her flowing dress and great bouquet, came and plucked Michael off the floor.

"Now we'll have them take one of just old friends." Her voice implied that this was best, most intimate of all. "Come here, Jebby, George—not you, Hamilton; this is just my friends—Sally—"

A little after that, what remained of formality disappeared and the hours flowed easily down the profuse stream of champagne. In the modern fashion, Hamilton Rutherford sat at the table with his arm about an old girl of his and assured his guests, which included not a few bewildered but enthusiastic Europeans, that the party was not nearly at an end; it was to reassemble at Zelli's after midnight. Michael saw Mrs. Dandy, not quite over her illness, rise to go and become caught in polite group after group, and he spoke of it to one of her daughters, who thereupon forcibly abducted her mother and called her car. Michael felt very considerate and proud of himself after having done this, and drank much more champagne.

"It's amazing," George Packman was telling him enthusiastically. "This show will cost Ham about five thousand dollars, and I understand they'll be just about his last. But did he countermand a bottle of champagne or a flower? Not he! He happens to have it—that young man. Do you know that T. G. Vance offered him a salary of fifty thousand dollars a year ten minutes before the wedding this morning? In another year he'll be back with the millionaires."

The conversation was interrupted by a plan to carry

Rutherford out on communal shoulders—a plan which six of them put into effect, and then stood in the four-o'clock sunshine waving good-bye to the bride and groom. But there must have been a mistake somewhere, for five minutes later Michael saw both bride and groom descending the stairway to the reception, each with a glass of champagne held defiantly on high.

"This is our way of doing things," he thought. "Generous and fresh and free; a sort of Virginia-plantation hospitality, but at a different pace now, nervous as a ticker tape."

Standing unself-consciously in the middle of the room to see which was the American ambassador, he realized with a start that he hadn't thought of Caroline in hours. He looked about him with a sort of alarm, and then he saw her across the room, very bright and young, and radiantly happy. He saw Rutherford near her, looking at her as if he could never look long enough, and as Michael watched them they seemed to recede as he had wished them to do that day in the Rue de Castiglione—recede and fade off into joys and griefs of their own, into the years that would take the toll of Rutherford's fine pride and Caroline's young, moving beauty; fade far away, so that now he could scarcely see them, as if they were shrouded in something as misty as her white billowing dress.

Michael was cured. The ceremonial function, with its pomp and revelry, had stood for a sort of initiation into a life where even his regret could not follow them. All the bitterness melted out of him suddenly and the world reconstituted itself out of the youth and happiness that was all around him, profligate as the spring sunshine. He was trying to remember which one of the bridesmaids he had made a date to dine with tonight as he walked forward to bid Hamilton and Caroline Rutherford good-by.

from

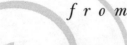

SENTIMENTAL
EDUCATION

GUSTAVE FLAUBERT

When the teen-aged hero of Sentimental Education,
*Frederick Moreau, falls desperately in love with
Madame Arnoux, she is a married woman with
children and his affections must go unreturned.
Years later he has the second chance every
unrequited lover dreams of, but as Flaubert
shows in this sharp little vignette,
timing is everything.*

He travelled.

He came to know the melancholy of the steamboat, the cold awakening in the tent, the tedium of landscapes and ruins, the bitterness of interrupted friendships.

He returned.

He went into society, and he had other loves. But the ever-present memory of the first made them insipid; and besides, the violence of desire, the very flower of feeling, had gone. His intellectual ambitions had also dwindled. Years went by; and he endured the idleness of his mind and the inertia of his heart.

Towards the end of March 1867, at nightfall, he was alone in his study when a woman came in.

'Madame Arnoux!'

'Frédéric!'

She seized him by the hands, drew him gently to the window, and gazed at him, saying:

'It's he! Yes, it's he!'

In the twilight he could see nothing but her eyes under the black lace veil which masked her face.

After placing a little red velvet wallet on the edge of the mantelpiece, she sat down. The two of them sat there, unable to speak, smiling at each other.

Finally he started asking all about herself and her husband.

They had settled in the depths of Brittany, so that they could live cheaply and pay off their debts. Arnoux was ill nearly all the time and looked like an old man now. His daughter was married and lived at Bordeaux, and her son was garrisoned at Mostaganem. Then she raised her head.

'But I've seen you again! I'm so happy!'

He did not fail to tell her that as soon as he had heard of the disaster which had overtaken them he had hurried round to their house.

'I know.'

'How?'

She had seen him in the courtyard, and had hidden.

'Why?'

Then, in a trembling voice, and with pauses between her words, she said:

'I was afraid. Yes . . . afraid of you . . . of myself!'

This revelation caused him a sort of paroxysm of delight. His heart beat wildly. She went on:

'Forgive me for not coming sooner.'

And pointing to the little red wallet, which was covered with golden palms, she said:

'I embroidered that specially for you. It contains the money for which the land at Belleville was supposed to be the security.'

Frédéric thanked her for the present, but reproached her for going to the trouble of bringing it personally.

'No. I didn't come for that. I looked forward so much to this visit, and now I shall go home . . . back there.'

And she told him about the place where she lived.

It was a low-built, single-storied house, with a garden full of huge box-trees and a double avenue of chestnuts stretching up to the top of the hill, from which there was a view of the sea.

'I go and sit there on a bench I call "Frédéric's bench".'

Then she started looking with greedy eyes at the furniture, the ornaments, and the pictures, in order to fix them in her memory. The portrait of the Marshal was half hidden by a curtain. But the golds and whites, standing out in the midst of the shadows, attracted her attention.

'I know that woman, don't I?'

'No, you can't!' said Frédéric. 'It's an old Italian painting.'

She confessed that she would like to go for a stroll through the streets on his arm.

They went out.

The lights of the shops illuminated intermittently her pale profile; then the darkness closed in on it again; and they moved among the carriages, the crowds, and the noise, oblivious of everything but themselves, hearing nothing, as if they had been walking together in the country, on a bed of dead leaves.

They talked about old times together, about the dinners in the days of *L'art Indusriel*, about Arnoux and his habit of tugging at the points of his collar and smearing pomade on his moustache, and about other things of a more profound and personal nature. What rapture he had felt the first time he had heard her sing! How beautiful she had been at Saint-Cloud on her name-day! He reminded her of the little garden at Auteuil, evenings at the theatre, an encounter on the boulevard, old servants, her negress.

She marvelled at his memory. But then she said:

'Sometimes your words come back to me like a distant echo, like the sound of a bell carried by the wind; and when I read about love in a book, I feel that you are there beside me.'

'You have made me feel all the things in books which people criticize as exaggerated,' said Frédéric. 'I can understand Werther not being put off by Charlotte's bread and butter.'

'My poor friend!'

She sighed, and after a long silence added:

'Never mind, we have loved each other well.'

'But without belonging to one another.'

'Perhaps it is better so,' she answered.

'No, no! How happy we should have been!'

'Yes, I can believe that, with a love like yours!'

It must have been very strong to survive so long a separation!

Frédéric asked her how she had discovered that he loved her.

'It was one evening when you kissed my wrist between

my glove and my sleeve. I said to myself: "Why, he loves me . . . he loves me." But I was afraid of making sure. Your discretion was so charming that I took pleasure in it as in an unconscious, never-failing homage.'

He regretted nothing. His former sufferings were redeemed.

When they returned, Madame Arnoux took off her hat. The lamp, standing on a console table, lit up her white hair. It was like a blow full in the chest.

To conceal his disappointment, he went down on his knees, took her hands, and started murmuring endearments to her.

'Your person, your slightest movements seemed to me to possess a superhuman importance in the world. My heart used to rise like the dust in your footsteps. The effect you had on me was that of a moonlit night in summer, when all is perfume, soft shadows, pale light, and infinite horizons. For me your name contained all the delights of flesh and spirit, and I repeated it again and again, trying to kiss it with my lips. I imagined nothing beyond your name. It conjured up Madame Arnoux, just as you were, with her two children, tender, serious, dazzlingly beautiful, and so kind-hearted! That picture blotted out all the others. Why, I didn't so much as give them a thought, since in the depths of myself I always had the music of your voice and the splendour of your eyes.'

She rapturously accepted this adoration of the woman she had ceased to be. Frédéric, drunk with his own eloquence, began to believe what he was saying. Madame Arnoux, with her back to the light, bent over him. He could feel the caress of her breath on his forehead, and the vague touch of her whole body through her clothes. They clasped hands; the toe of her shoe protruded a little from under her dress, and almost fainting with emotion, he said to her:

'The sight of your foot disturbs me.'

An impulse of modesty made her get up. Then, motionless, and talking with the strange intonation of a sleepwalker, she said:

'At my age! Him! Frédéric! . . . No woman has ever been loved as I have been loved. No, no! What's the use of being young? I don't care about youth. I despise all the women who come here!'

'Oh, hardly any do,' he said, to please her.

Her face lit up, and she asked if he intended to marry.

He swore he never would.

'Really and truly? Why not?'

'Because of you,' said Frédéric, clasping her in his arms.

She stood there, leaning backwards, her lips parted, her eyes raised. Suddenly she pushed him away with a look of despair; and when he begged her to speak, she bowed her head and said:

'I should have liked to make you happy.'

Frédéric suspected that Madame Arnoux had come to offer herself to him; and once again he was filled with desire, a frenzied, rabid lust such as he had never known before. Yet he also had another, indefinable feeling, a repugnance akin to a dread of committing incest. Another fear restrained him—the fear of being disgusted later. Besides, what a nuisance it would be! And partly out of prudence and partly to avoid degrading his ideal, he turned on his heel and started rolling a cigarette.

She gazed at him admiringly.

'How considerate you are! There's nobody like you! There's nobody like you!'

Eleven o'clock struck.

'Already!' she said. 'At a quarter past, I shall go.'

She sat down again; but she watched the clock, while he went on walking up and down and smoking. Neither of them could think of anything more to say. In every parting there comes a moment when the beloved is already no longer with us.

At last, when the minute-hand pointed to a little after twenty-five past, she slowly picked up her hat by the ribbons.

'Good-bye, my friend, my dear friend! I shall never see you again. This was my last act as a woman. My soul will never leave you. May all the blessings of heaven be upon you!'

And she kissed him on the forehead like a mother.

But she seemed to be looking for something, and finally she asked him for some scissors.

She took out her comb, and all her white hair fell over her shoulders.

With an abrupt gesture she cut off a long lock close to her head.

'Keep it. Good-bye!'

When she had gone out, Frédéric opened his window. On the pavement Madame Arnoux beckoned to a passing cab. She got in. The carriage disappeared.

And that was all.

from

SWANN'S WAY

MARCEL PROUST

*Few things are as exhilarating as realizing what a fool
you've been. Though cheated on and dumped by his selfish paramour Odette d'Crecy, the elegant Charles Swann
finally wakes up to the world that he's ignored while in
her company. No one describes love's intricate and dev-
astating paths as well as Marcel Proust, and the
moment of mental sunrise he portrays here
stands as one of the greatest inspirations
to those trying to rediscover love.*

He went to see Odette. He sat down at a distance from her. He did not dare to embrace her, not knowing whether it would be affection or anger that a kiss would provoke, either in her or in himself. He sat there silent, watching their love expire. Suddenly he made up his mind.

"Odette, my darling," he began, "I know I'm being simply odious, but I must ask you a few questions. You remember the idea I once had about you and Mme Verdurin? Tell me, was it true? Have you, with her or anyone else, ever?"

She shook her head, pursing her lips, a sign which people commonly employ to signify that they are not going, because it would bore them to go, when someone has asked, "Are you coming to watch the procession go by?", or "Will you be at the review?". But this shake of the head thus normally applied to an event that has yet to come, imparts for that reason an element of uncertainty to the denial of an event that is past. Furthermore, it suggests reasons of personal propriety only, rather than of disapprobation or moral impossibility. When he saw Odette thus signal to him that the insinuation was false, Swann realised that it was quite possibly true.

"I've told you, no. You know quite well," she added, seeming angry and uncomfortable.

"Yes, I know, but are you quite sure? Don't say to me,

'You know quite well'; say, 'I have never done anything of that sort with any woman.'"

She repeated his words like a lesson learned by rote, in a sarcastic tone, and as though she hoped thereby to be rid of him: "I have never done anything of that sort with any woman."

"Can you swear to me on the medal of Our Lady of Laghet?"

Swann knew that Odette would never perjure herself on that.

"Oh, you do make me so miserable," she cried, with a jerk of her body as though to shake herself free of the constraint of his question. "Haven't you had enough? What's the matter with you to-day? You seem determined to make me hate you. I wanted to be friends with you again, for us to have a nice time together, like the old days; and this is all the thanks I get!"

However, he would not let her go but sat there like a surgeon waiting for a spasm to subside that has interrupted his operation but will not make him abandon it.

"You're quite wrong to suppose that I'd bear you the least ill-will in the world, Odette," he said to her with a persuasive and deceitful gentleness. "I never speak to you except of what I already know, and I always know a great deal more than I say. But you alone can mitigate by your confession what makes me hate you so long as it has been reported to me only by other people. My anger with you has nothing to do with your actions—I can and do forgive you everything because I love you—but with your untruthfulness, the ridiculous untruthfulness which makes you persist in denying things which I know to be true. How can you expect me to go on loving you when I see you maintain, when I hear you swear to me a thing which I know to be false? Odette, don't prolong this moment which is agony for us both. If you want to, you can end it in a second, you'll be free of it for ever. Tell me, on your medal, yes or no, whether you have ever done these things."

"How on earth do I know?" she exclaimed angrily. "Perhaps I have, ever so long ago, when I didn't know what I was doing, perhaps two or three times."

Swann had prepared himself for every possibility. Reality must therefore be something that bears no relation to possibilities, any more than the stab of a knife in one's body bears to the gradual movement of the clouds overhead, since those words, "two or three times," carved as it were a cross upon the living tissues of his heart. Strange indeed that those words, "two or three times," nothing more than words, words uttered in the air, at a distance, could so lacerate a man's heart, as if they had actually pierced it, could make a man ill, like a poison he has drunk. Instinctively Swann thought of the remark he had heard at Mme de Saint-Euverte's: "I've never seen anything to beat it since the table-turning." The agony that he now suffered in no way resembled what he had supposed.

Not only because, even in his moments of most complete distrust, he had rarely imagined such an extremity of evil, but because, even when he did try to imagine this thing, it remained vague, uncertain, was not clothed in the particular horror which had sprung from the words "perhaps two or three times," was not armed with that specific cruelty, as different from anything that he had known as a disease by which one is struck down for the first time. And yet this Odette from whom all this evil sprang was no less dear to him, was, on the contrary, more precious, as if, in proportion as his sufferings increased, the price of the sedative, of the antidote which this woman alone possessed, increased at the same time. He wanted to devote more care to her, as one tends a disease which one has suddenly discovered to be more serious. He wanted the horrible things which, she had told him, she had done "two or three times," not to happen again. To ensure that, he must watch over Odette. People often say that, by pointing out to a man the faults of his mistress, you succeed only in strengthening his attachment to her, because he does not believe you; yet how much more if he does! But, Swann asked himself, how could he manage to protect her? He might perhaps be able to preserve her from the contamination of a particular woman, but there were hundreds of others; and he realised what madness had come over him when, on the evening when he had failed to find Odette at the Verdurins', he had begun to desire the possession—as if that were ever possible—of another person. Happily for Swann, beneath the mass of new sufferings which had entered his soul like an invading horde, there lay a natural foundation, older, more placid, and silently industrious, like the cells of an injured organ which at once set to work to repair the damaged tissues, or the muscles of a paralysed limb which tend to recover their former movements. These older, more autochthonous inhabitants of his soul absorbed all Swann's strength, for a while, in that obscure task of reparation which gives one an illusory sense of repose during convalescence, or after an operation. This time it was not so much—as it ordinarily was—in Swann's brain that this slackening of tension due to exhaustion took effect, it was rather in his heart. But all the things in life that have once existed tend to recur, and like a dying animal stirred once more by the throes of a convulsion which seemed to have ended, upon Swann's heart, spared for a moment only, the same agony returned of its own accord to trace the same cross. He remembered those moonlit evenings, when, leaning back in the victoria that was taking him to the Rue La Pérouse, he would wallow voluptuously in the emotions of a man in love, oblivious of the poisoned fruit that such emotions must inevitably bear. But all those thoughts lasted for no more than a second, the time that it took him to press his hand to his heart, to draw breath again and to contrive to smile, in order to hide his torment. Already he had begun to put further questions. For his jealousy, which had taken more pains than any enemy would have done to strike him this savage blow, to make him forcibly acquainted with the most cruel suffering he had ever known, his jealousy was not satisfied that he had yet suffered enough, and sought to expose him to an even deeper wound. Thus, like an evil deity, his jealousy inspired Swann, driving him on towards his ruin. It was not his fault, but Odette's alone, if at first his torment was not exacerbated.

"My darling," he began again, "it's all over now. Was it with anyone I know?"

"No, I swear it wasn't. Besides, I think I exaggerated, I never really went as far as that."

He smiled, and went on: "Just as you like. It doesn't really matter, but it's a pity that you can't give me the name. If I were able to form an idea of the person it would prevent my ever thinking of her again. I say it for your sake, because then I shouldn't bother you any more about it. It's so calming to be able to form a clear picture of things in one's mind. What is really terrible is what one can't imagine. But you've been so sweet to me; I don't want to tire you. I do thank you with all my heart for all the good that you've done me. I've quite finished now. Only one word more: how long ago?"

"Oh, Charles, can't you see you're killing me? It's all so long ago. I've never given it a thought. Anyone would think you were positively trying to put those ideas into my head again. A lot of good that would do you!" she concluded, with unconscious stupidity but intentional malice.

"Oh, I only wanted to know whether it had been since I've known you. It's only natural. Did it happen here? You can't give me any particular evening, so that I can remind myself what I was doing at the time? You must realise that it's not possible that you don't remember with whom, Odette, my love."

"But I don't know; really, I don't. I think it was in the Bois, one evening when you came to meet us on the Island. You'd been dining with the Princesse des Laumes," she added, happy to be able to furnish him with a precise detail which testified to her veracity. "There was a woman at the next table whom I hadn't seen for ages. She said to me, 'Come round behind the rock, there, and look at the moonlight on the water!' At first I just yawned, and said, 'No, I'm too tired, and I'm quite happy where I am, thank you.' She assured me there'd never been any moonlight to touch it. 'I've heard that tale before,' I said to her. I knew quite well what she was after."

Odette narrated this episode almost with a smile, either because it appeared to her to be quite natural, or because she thought she was thereby minimising its importance, or else so as not to appear humiliated. But, catching sight of Swann's face, she changed her tone:

"You're a fiend! You enjoy torturing me, making me tell you lies, just so that you'll leave me in peace."

This second blow was even more terrible for Swann than

the first. Never had he supposed it to have been so recent an event, hidden from his eyes that had been too innocent to discern it, not in a past which he had never known, but in the course of evenings which he so well remembered, which he had lived through with Odette, of which he had supposed himself to have such an intimate, such an exhaustive knowledge, and which now assumed, retrospectively, an aspect of ugliness and deceit. In the midst of them, suddenly, a gaping chasm had opened: that moment on the island in the Bois de Boulogne. Without being intelligent, Odette had the charm of naturalness. She had recounted, she had acted the little scene with such simplicity that Swann, as he gasped for breath, could vividly see it: Odette yawning, the "rock, there," . . . He could hear her answer—alas, how gaily—"I've heard that tale before!" He felt that she would tell him nothing more that evening, that no further revelation was to be expected for the present. He was silent for a time, then said to her:

"My poor darling, you must forgive me; I know I've distressed you, but it's all over now; I won't think of it any more."

But she saw that his eyes remained fixed upon the things that he did not know, and on that past era of their love, monotonous and soothing in his memory because it was vague, and now rent, as with a gaping wound, by that moment on the Island in the Bois, by moonlight, after his dinner with the Princesse des Laumes. But he was so imbued with the habit of finding life interesting—of marvelling at the strange discoveries that there are to be made in it—that even while he was suffering so acutely that he did not believe he could bear such agony much longer, he was saying to himself: "Life is really astonishing, and holds some fine surprises; it appears that vice is far more common than one has been led to believe. Here is a woman I trusted, who seems so simple, so straightforward, who, in any case, even allowing that her morals are not strict, seemed quite normal and healthy in her tastes and inclinations. On the basis of a most improbable accusation, I question her, and the little that she admits reveals far more than I could ever have suspected." But he could not confine himself to these detached observations. He sought to form an exact estimate of the significance of what she had just told him, in order to decide whether she had done these things often and was likely to do them again. He repeated her words to himself: "I knew quite well what she was after." "Two or three times." "I've heard that tale before." But they did not reappear in his memory unarmed; each of them still held its knife, with which it stabbed him anew. For a long time, like a sick man who cannot restrain himself from attempting every minute to make the movement that he knows will hurt him, he kept on murmuring to himself: "I'm quite happy where I am, thank you," "I've heard that tale before," but the pain was so intense that he was obliged to stop. He was amazed to find that acts which he had always hitherto judged so lightly, had dismissed, indeed, with a laugh, should have become as serious to him as a disease which may prove fatal. He knew any number of women whom he could ask to keep an eye on Odette, but how was he to expect them to adjust themselves to his new point of view, and not to look at the matter from the one which for so long had been his own, which had always guided him in sexual matters; not to say to him with a laugh: "You jealous monster, wanting to rob other people of their pleasure!" By what trap-door suddenly lowered had he (who had never had hitherto from his love for Odette any but the most refined pleasures) been precipitated into this new circle of hell from which he could not see how he was ever to escape. Poor Odette! He did not hold it against her. She was only half to blame. Had he not been told that it was her own mother who had sold her, when she was still hardly more than a child, at Nice, to a wealthy Englishman? But what an agonising truth was now contained for him in those lines of Alfred de Vigny's *Journal d'un Poète* which he had previously read without emotion: "When one feels oneself smitten by love for a woman, one should say to oneself, 'Who are the people around her? What kind of life has she led?' All one's future happiness lies in the answer." Swann was astonished that such simple sentences, spelt over in his mind, as "I've heard that tale before" or "I knew quite well what she was after," could cause him so much pain. But he realised that

what he thought of as simple sentences were in fact the components of the framework which still enclosed, and could
inflict on him again, the anguish he had felt while Odette
was telling her story. For it was indeed the same anguish
that he now was feeling anew. For all that he now knew—
for all that, as time went on, he might even have partly
forgotten and forgiven—whenever he repeated her words
his old anguish refashioned him as he had been before
Odette had spoken: ignorant, trustful; his merciless jealousy
placed him once again, so that he might be pierced by
Odette's admission, in the position of a man who does not
yet know; and after several months this old story would still
shatter him like a sudden revelation. He marvelled at the terrible recreative power of his memory. It was only by the
weakening of that generative force, whose fecundity dimin-
ishes with age, that he could hope for a relaxation of his tor-
ments. But, as soon as the power of any one of Odette's
remarks to make Swann suffer seemed to be nearly exhausted,
lo and behold another, one of those to which he had hitherto
paid little attention, almost a new observation, came to rein-
force the others and to strike at him with undiminished force.
The memory of the evening on which he had dined with the
Princesse des Laumes was painful to him, but it was no more
than the centre, the core of his pain, which radiated vaguely
round about it, overflowing into all the preceding and following days. And on whatever point in it his memory sought

to linger, it was the whole of that season, during which the Verdurins had so often gone to dine on the Island in the Bois, that racked him. So violently that by slow degrees the curiosity which his jealousy aroused in him was neutralised by his fear of the fresh tortures he would be inflicting upon himself were he to satisfy it. He recognised that the entire period of Odette's life which had elapsed before she first met him, a period of which he had never sought to form a picture in his mind, was not the featureless abstraction which he could vaguely see, but had consisted of so many definite, dated years, each crowded with concrete incidents. But were he to learn more of them, he feared lest that past of hers, colourless, fluid and supportable, might assume a tangible and monstrous form, an individual and diabolical countenance. And he continued to refrain from seeking to visualise it, no longer from laziness of mind, but from fear of suffering. He hoped that, some day, he might be able to hear the Island in the Bois or the Princesse des Laumes mentioned without feeling any twinge of the old heartache; and meanwhile he thought it imprudent to provoke Odette into furnishing him with new facts, the names of more places and different circumstances which, when his malady was still scarcely healed, would revive it again in another form.

But, often enough, the things that he did know, that he dreaded, now, to learn, were revealed to him by Odette herself, spontaneously and unwittingly; for the gap which her vices made between her actual life and the comparatively innocent life which Swann had believed, and often still believed his mistress to lead, was far wider than she knew. A vicious person, always affecting the same air of virtue before people whom he is anxious to keep from having any suspicion of his vices, has no gauge at hand from which to ascertain how far those vices, whose continuous growth is imperceptible to himself, have gradually segregated him from the normal ways of life. In the course of their cohabitation, in Odette's mind, side by side with the memory of those of her actions which she concealed from Swann, others were gradually coloured, infected by them, without her being able to detect anything strange in them, without their causing any jarring note in the particular surroundings which they occupied in her inner world; but if she related them to Swann, he was shattered by the revelation of the way of life to which they pointed. One day he was trying—without hurting Odette—to discover from her whether she had ever had any dealings with procuresses. He was, as a matter of fact, convinced that she had not; the anonymous letter had put the idea into his mind, but in a mechanical way; it had met with no credence there, but for all that had remained, and Swann, wishing to be rid of the purely material but none the less burdensome presence of the suspicion, hoped that Odette would now extirpate it for ever.

"Oh, no! . . . Not that they don't pester me," she added

with a smile of self-satisfied vanity, quite unaware that it could not appear justifiable to Swann. "There was one of them waited more than two hours for me yesterday—offered me any money I asked. It seems there's an ambassador who said to her, 'I'll kill myself if you don't bring her to me'— meaning me! They told her I'd gone out, but she waited and waited, and in the end I had to go and speak to her myself before she'd go away. I wish you could have seen the way I went for her; my maid could hear me from the next room and told me I was shouting at the top of my voice: 'But haven't I told you I don't want to! It's just the way I feel. I should hope I'm still free to do as I please! If I needed the money, I could understand . . .' The porter has orders not to let her in again; he's to tell her I'm out of town. Oh, I wish I could have had you hidden somewhere in the room while I was talking to her. I know you'd have been pleased, my darling. There's some good in your little Odette, you see, after all, though people do say such dreadful things about her."

Besides, her very admissions—when she made any—of faults which she supposed him to have discovered, served Swann as a starting-point for new doubt rather than putting an end to the old. For her admissions never exactly coincided with his doubts. In vain might Odette expurgate her confession of all its essentials, there would remain in the accessories something which Swann had never yet imagined, which crushed him anew, and would enable him to alter the terms of the problem of his jealousy. And these admissions he could never forget. His soul carried them along, cast them aside, then cradled them again in its bosom, like corpses in a river. And they poisoned it.

She spoke to him once of a visit that Forcheville had paid her on the day of the Paris-Murcie Fête. "What! you knew him as long ago as that? Oh, yes, of course you did," he corrected himself, so as not to show that he had been ignorant of the fact. And suddenly he began to tremble at the thought that, on the day of the Paris-Murcie Fête, when he had received from her the letter which he had so carefully preserved, she had perhaps been having lunch with Forcheville at the Maison d'Or. She swore that she had not. "Still, the Maison d'Or reminds me of something or other which I knew at the time wasn't true," he pursued, hoping to frighten her. "Yes, that I hadn't been there at all that evening when I told you I had just come from there, and you'd been looking for me at Prévost's," she replied (judging by his manner that he knew) with a firmness that was based not so much on cynicism as on timidity, a fear of offending Swann which her own self-respect made her anxious to conceal, and a desire to show him that she could be perfectly frank if she chose. And so she struck with all the precision and force of a headsman wielding his axe, and yet could not be charged with cruelty since she was quite unconscious of hurting him; she even laughed, though perhaps, it is true, chiefly in order not to appear chastened or embarrassed. "It's quite true, I hadn't been to the Maison Dorée. I was coming away from Forcheville's. I really had been to Prévost's—I didn't make that up—and he met me there and asked me to come in and look at his prints. But someone else came to see him. I told you I'd come from the Maison d'Or because I was afraid you might be angry with me. It was rather nice of me, really, don't you see? Even if I did wrong, at least I'm telling you all about it now, aren't I? What would I have to gain by not telling you that I lunched with him on the day of the Paris-Murcie Fête, if it was true? Especially as at the time we didn't know one another quite so well as we do now, did we, darling?"

He smiled back at her with the sudden, craven weakness of the shattered creature which these crushing words had made of him. So, even in the months of which he had never dared to think again because they had been too happy, in those months when she had loved him, she was already lying to him! Besides that moment (that first evening on which they had "done a cattleya") when she had told him that she was coming from the Maison Dorée, how many others must there have been, each of them also concealing a falsehood of which Swann had had no suspicion. He recalled how she had said to him once: "I need only tell Mme Verdurin that my dress wasn't ready, or that my cab came late. There's always some excuse." From himself too, probably, many a time when she had glibly uttered such words as explain a delay or justify an alteration of the hour fixed for a meeting, they must have hidden, without his having the least inkling of it at the time, an appointment she had with some other man, some man to whom she had said: "I need only tell Swann that my dress wasn't ready, or that my cab came late. There's always some excuse." And beneath all his most tender memories, beneath the simplest words that Odette had spoken to him in those early days, words which he had believed as though they were gospel, beneath the daily actions which she had recounted to him, beneath the most ordinary places, her dressmaker's flat, the Avenue du Bois, the race-course, he could feel (dissembled by virtue of that temporal superfluity which, even in days that have been most circumstantially accounted for, still leaves a margin of room that may serve as a hiding place for certain unconfessed actions), he could feel the insinuation of a possible undercurrent of falsehood which rendered ignoble all that had remained most precious to him (his happiest evenings, the Rue La Pérouse itself, which Odette must constantly have been leaving at other hours than those of which she told him) everywhere disseminating something of the shadowy horror that had gripped him when he had heard her admission with regard to the Maison Dorée, and, like the obscene creatures in the "Desolation of Nineveh," shattering stone by stone the whole edifice of his past . . . . If, now, he turned away whenever his memory repeated the cruel name of the Maison Dorée, it was because that name recalled to him no longer, as, but recently, at Mme de Saint-Euverte's party, a happiness which he had long since lost, but a misfortune of which he had just become aware. Then it happened with the Maison Dorée as it had happened with the Island in the Bois, that gradually its name ceased to trouble him. For what we suppose to be our love or our jealousy is never a single, continuous and indivisible passion. It is composed of an infinity of successive loves, of different jealousies, each of which is ephemeral, although by their uninterrupted multiplicity they give us the impression of continuity, the illusion of unity. The life of Swann's love, the fidelity of his jealousy, were formed of the death, the infidelity, of innumerable desires, innumerable doubts, all of which had Odette for their object. If he had remained for any length of time without seeing her, those that died would not have been replaced by others. But the presence of Odette continued to sow in Swann's heart alternate seeds of love and suspicion.

On certain evenings she would suddenly resume towards him an amenity of which she would warn him sternly that he must take immediate advantage, under penalty of not seeing it repeated for years to come; he must instantly accompany her home, to "do a cattleya," and the desire which she claimed to have for him was so sudden, so inexplicable, so imperious, the caresses which she lavished on him were so demonstrative and so unwonted, that this brutal and improbable fondness made Swann just as unhappy as any lie or unkindness. One evening when he had thus, in obedience to her command, gone home with her, and she was interspersing her kisses with passionate words, in strange contrast to her habitual coldness, he suddenly thought he heard a sound; he rose, searched everywhere and found nobody, but hadn't the heart to return to his place by her side; whereupon, in the height of fury, she broke a vase and said to him: "One can never do anything right with you!" And he was left uncertain whether she had not actually had some man concealed in the room, whose jealousy she had wished to exacerbate or his senses to inflame.

Sometimes he repaired to brothels in the hope of learning something about Odette, although he dared not mention her name. "I have a little thing you're sure to like," the "manageress" would greet him, and he would stay for an hour or so chatting gloomily to some poor girl who sat there astonished that he went no further. One of them, who was quite young and very pretty, said to him once: "Of course, what I'd like would be to find a real friend—then he might be quite certain I'd never go with any other men again."

"Really, do you think it possible for a woman to be touched by a man's loving her, and never to be unfaithful to him?" asked Swann anxiously.

"Why, of course! It all depends on people's characters!"

Swann could not help saying to these girls the sort of things that would have delighted the Princesse des Laumes.

To the one who was in search of a friend he said with a smile: "But how nice, you've put on blue eyes to go with your sash."

"And you too, you've got blue cuffs on."

"What a charming conversation we're having for a place of this sort! I'm not boring you, am I; or keeping you?"

"No, I'm not in a hurry. If you'd have bored me I'd have said so. But I like hearing you talk."

"I'm very flattered . . . . Aren't we having a nice chat?" he asked the "manageress," who had just looked in.

"Why, yes, that's just what I was saying to myself, how good they're being! But there it is! People come to my house now just to talk. The Prince was telling me only the other day that it's far nicer here than at home with his wife. It seems that, nowadays, all the society ladies are so flighty; a real scandal, I call it. But I'll leave you in peace now," she ended discreetly, and left Swann with the girl who had the blue eyes. But presently he rose and said good-bye to her. She had ceased to interest him. She did not know Odette.

The painter having been ill, Dr. Cottard recommended a sea-voyage. Several of the "faithful" spoke of accompanying him. The Verdurins could not face the prospect of being left alone in Paris, so first of all hired and finally purchased a yacht; thus Odette went on frequent cruises. Whenever she had been away for any length of time, Swann would feel that he was beginning to detach himself from her, but as though this moral distance were proportionate to the physical dis-

tance between them, whenever he heard that Odette had
returned to Paris, he could not rest without seeing her. Once,
when they had gone away ostensibly for a month only, either
they succumbed to a series of temptations, or else M.
Verdurin had cunningly arranged everything beforehand to
please his wife, and disclosed his plans to the "faithful" only
as time went on; at all events, from Algiers they flitted to
Tunis; then to Italy, Greece, Constantinople, Asia Minor.
They had been absent for nearly a year, and Swann felt perfectly at ease and almost happy. Although Mme Verdurin had
endeavoured to persuade the pianist and Dr. Cottard that
their respective aunt and patients had no need of them, and
that in any event it was most rash to allow Mme Cottard to
return to Paris which, so M. Verdurin affirmed, was in the
throes of revolution, she was obliged to grant them their liberty at Constantinople. And the painter came home with
them. One day, shortly after the return of these four travellers,
Swann, seeing an omnibus for the Luxembourg approaching
and having some business there, had jumped on it and found
himself sitting opposite Mme Cottard, who was paying a
round of visits to people whose "day" it was, in full fig, with
a plume in her hat, a silk dress, a muff, an umbrella-sunshade,
a card-case, and a pair of white gloves fresh from the clean-
ers. Clothed in these regalia, she would, in fine weather, go on
foot from one house to another in the same neighborhood,
but when she had to proceed to another district, would make

use of a transfer-ticket on the omnibus. For the first minute or two, until the natural amiability of the woman broke through the starched surface of the doctor's-wife, not being certain, moreover, whether she ought to talk to Swann about the Verdurins, she proceeded to hold forth, in her slow, awkward and soft-spoken voice, which every now and then was completely drowned by the rattling of the omnibus, on topics selected from those which she had picked up and would repeat in each of the score of houses up the stairs of which she clambered in the course of an afternoon.

"I needn't ask you, M. Swann, whether a man so much in the swim as yourself has been to the Mirlitons to see the portrait by Machard which the whole of Paris is rushing to see. Well and what do you think of it? Whose camp are you in, those who approve or those who don't? It's the same in every house in Paris now, no one talks about anything else but Machard's portrait. You aren't smart, you aren't really cultured, you aren't up-to-date unless you give an opinion on Machard's portrait."

Swann having replied that he had not seen this portrait, Mme Cottard was afraid that she might have hurt his feelings by obliging him to confess the omission.

"Oh, that's quite all right! At least you admit it frankly. You don't consider yourself disgraced because you haven't seen Machard's portrait. I find that most commendable. Well now, I have seen it. Opinion is divided, you know, there are some people who find it a bit over-finical, like whipped cream, they say; but I think it's just ideal. Of course, she's not a bit like the blue and yellow ladies of our friend Biche. But I must tell you quite frankly (you'll think me dreadfully old-fashioned, but I always say just what I think), that I don't understand his work. I can quite see the good points in his portrait of my husband, oh, dear me, yes, and it's certainly less odd than most of what he does, but even then he had to give the poor man a blue moustache! But Machard! Just listen to this now, the husband of the friend I'm on my way to see at this very moment (which has given me the very great pleasure of your company), has promised her that if he is elected to the Academy (he's one of the Doctor's colleagues) he'll get Machard to paint her portrait. *There's* something to look forward to! I have another friend who insists that she'd rather have Leloir. I'm only a wretched Philistine, and for all I know Leloir may be technically superior to Machard. But I do think that the most important thing about a portrait, especially when it's going to cost ten thousand francs, is that it should be like, and a pleasant likeness if you know what I mean."

Having exhausted this topic, to which she had been inspired by the loftiness of her plume, the monogram on her card-case, the little number inked inside each of her gloves by the cleaner, and the embarrassment of speaking to Swann about the Verdurins, Mme Cottard, seeing that they had still a long way to go before they would reach the corner of the

Rue Bonaparte where the conductor was to set her down, listened to the promptings of her heart, which counselled other words than these.

"Your ears must have been burning," she ventured, "while we were on the yacht with Mme Verdurin. We talked about you all the time."

Swann was genuinely astonished, for he supposed that his name was never uttered in the Verdurins' presence.

"You see," Mme Cottard went on, "Mme de Crécy was there; need I say more? Wherever Odette is, it's never long before she begins talking about you. And you can imagine that it's never unfavourably. What, you don't believe me!" she went on, noticing that Swann looked sceptical.

And, carried away by the sincerity of her conviction, without putting any sly meaning into the word, which she used purely in the sense in which one employs it to speak of the affection that unites a pair of friends: "Why, she *adores* you! No, indeed, I'm sure it would never do to say anything against you when she was about; one would soon be put in one's place! Whatever we might be doing, if we were looking at a picture, for instance, she would say, 'If only we had him here, he's the man who could tell us whether it's genuine or not. There's no one like him for that.' And all day long she would be saying, 'What can he be doing just now? I do hope he's doing a little work! It's too dreadful that a fellow with such gifts as he has should be so lazy.' (Forgive me, won't you.) 'I can see him this very moment; he's thinking of us, he's wondering where we are.' Indeed, she made a remark which I found absolutely charming. M. Verdurin asked her, 'How in the world can you see what he's doing, when he's a thousand miles away?' And Odette answered, 'Nothing is impossible to the eye of a friend.' No, I assure you, I'm not saying it just to flatter you; you have a true friend in her, such as one doesn't often find. I can tell you, besides, that if you don't know it you're the only one who doesn't. Mme Verdurin told me as much herself on our last day with them (one talks freely, don't you know, before a parting), 'I don't say that Odette isn't fond of us, but anything that we may say to her counts for very little beside what Swann might say.' Oh, mercy, there's the conductor stopping for me. Here I've been chatting away to you, and would have gone right past the Rue Bonaparte and never noticed . . . . Will you be so very kind as to tell me if my plume is straight?"

And Mme Cottard withdrew from her muff, to offer it to Swann, a white-gloved hand from which there floated, together with a transfer-ticket, a vision of high life that pervaded the omnibus, blended with the fragrance of newly cleaned kid. And Swann felt himself overflowing with affection towards her, as well as towards Mme Verdurin (and almost towards Odette, for the feeling that he now entertained for her, being no longer tinged with pain, could scarcely be described, now, as love) as from the platform of the omnibus he followed her with fond eyes as she gallantly threaded her way along the Rue Bonaparte, her plume erect, her skirt held up in one hand, while in the other she clasped her umbrella and her card-case with its monogram exposed to view, her muff dancing up and down in front of her as she went.

To counterbalance the morbid feelings that Swann cherished for Odette, Mme Cottard, a wiser physician, in this case, than ever her husband would have been, had grafted on to them others more normal, feelings of gratitude, of friendship, which in Swann's mind would make Odette seem more human (more like other women, since other women could inspire the same feelings in him), would hasten her final transformation back into the Odette, loved with an undisturbed affection, who had taken him home one evening after a revel at the painter's to drink a glass of orangeade with Forcheville, the Odette with whom Swann had glimpsed the possibility of living in happiness.

In the past, having often thought with terror that a day must come when he would cease to be in love with Odette, he had determined to keep a sharp look-out, and as soon as he felt that love was beginning to leave him, to cling to it and hold it back. But now, to the diminution of his love there corresponded a simultaneous diminution in his desire to remain in love. For a man cannot change, that is to say become another person, while continuing to obey the dictates of the self which he has ceased to be. Occasionally the name glimpsed in a newspaper, of one of the men whom he supposed to have been Odette's lovers, reawakened his jealousy. But it was very mild, and, inasmuch as it proved to him that he had not completely emerged from that period in which he had so greatly suffered—but in which he had also known so voluptuous a way of feeling—and that the hazards of the road ahead might still enable him to catch an occasional furtive, distant glimpse of its beauties, this jealousy gave him, if anything, an agreeable thrill, as, to the sad Parisian who is leaving Venice behind him to return to France, a last mosquito proves that Italy and summer are still not too remote. But, as a rule, with this particular period of his life from which he was emerging, when he made an effort, if not to remain in it, at least to obtain a clear view of it while he still could, he discovered that already it was too late; he would have liked to glimpse, as though it were a landscape that was about to disappear, that love from which he had departed; but it is so difficult to enter into a state of duality and to present to oneself the lifelike spectacle of a feeling one has ceased to possess, that very soon, the clouds gathering in his brain, he could see nothing at all, abandoned the attempt, took the glasses from his nose and wiped them; and he told himself that he would do better to rest for a little, that there would be time enough later on, and settled back into his corner with the incuriosity, the torpor of the drowsy traveller who pulls his hat down over his eyes to get some sleep in the railway-carriage that is drawing him, he feels, faster and faster out of the country in which he has lived for so long and which he had vowed not to allow to slip away from him without looking out to bid it a last farewell. Indeed, like the same traveller if he does not awake until he has crossed the frontier and is back in France, when Swann chanced to alight, close at hand, on proof that Forcheville had been Odette's lover, he realised that it caused him no pain, that love was now far behind, and he regretted that he had had no warning of the moment when he had emerged from it for ever. And just as, before kissing Odette for the first time, he had sought to imprint upon his memory the face that for so long had been familiar before it was altered by the additional memory of their kiss, so he could have wished—in thought at least—to have been able to bid farewell, while she still existed, to the Odette who had aroused his love and jealousy, to the Odette who had caused him to suffer, and whom now he would never see again.

He was mistaken. He was destined to see her once again, a few weeks later. It was while he was asleep, in the twilight of a dream. He was walking with Mme Verdurin, Dr. Cottard, a young man in a fez whom he failed to identify, the painter, Odette, Napoleon III and my grandfather, along a path which followed the line of the coast, and overhung the sea, now at a great height, now by a few feet only, so that they were continually going up and down. Those of the party who had reached the downward slope were no longer visible to those who were still climbing; what little daylight yet remained was failing, and it seemed as though they were about to be shrouded in darkness. From time to time the waves dashed against the edge, and Swann could feel on his cheek a shower of freezing spray. Odette told him to wipe it off, but he could not, and felt confused and helpless in her company, as well as because he was in his nightshirt. He hoped that, in the darkness, this might pass unnoticed; Mme Verdurin, however, fixed her astonished gaze upon him for an endless moment, during which he saw her face change shape, her nose grow longer, while beneath it there sprouted a heavy moustache. He turned round to look at Odette; her cheeks were pale, with little red spots, her features drawn and ringed with shadows; but she looked back at him with eyes welling with affection, ready to detach themselves like tears and to fall upon his face, and he felt that he loved her so much that he would have liked to carry her off with him at once. Suddenly Odette turned her wrist, glanced at a tiny watch, and said: "I must go." She took leave of everyone in the same formal manner, without taking Swann aside, without telling him where they were to meet that evening, or next day. He dared not ask; he would have liked to follow her, but he was obliged, without turning back in her direction, to answer with a smile some question from Mme Verdurin; but his heart was frantically beating, he felt that he now hated Odette, he would gladly have gouged out those eyes which a moment ago he had loved so much, have crushed those flaccid cheeks. He continued to climb with Mme Verdurin, that is to say to draw further away with each step from Odette, who was going downhill in the other direction. A second passed and it was many hours since she had left them. The painter remarked to Swann that Napoleon III had slipped away immediately after Odette. "They had obviously arranged it between them," he added. "They must have met at the foot of the cliff, but they didn't want to say good-bye together because of appearances. She is his mistress." The strange young man burst into tears. Swann tried to console him. "After all, she's quite right," he said to the young man, drying his eyes for him and taking off the fez to make him feel more at ease. "I've advised her to do it dozens of times. Why be so distressed? He was obviously the man to understand her." So Swann reasoned with himself, for the young man whom he had failed at first to identify was himself too; like certain novelists, he had distributed his own personality between two characters, the one who was dreaming the dream, and another whom he saw in front of him sporting a fez.

As for Napoleon III, it was to Forcheville that some vague association of ideas, then a certain modification of the baron's usual physiognomy, and lastly the broad ribbon of the Legion of Honour across his breast, had made Swann give that name; in reality, and in everything that the person who appeared in his dream represented and recalled to him, it was indeed Forcheville. For, from an incomplete and changing set of images, Swann in his sleep drew false deductions, enjoying at the same time, momentarily, such a creative power that he was able to reproduce himself by a simple act of division, like certain lower organisms; with the warmth that he felt in his own palm he modelled the hollow of a strange hand which he thought he was clasping, and out of feelings and impressions of which he was not yet conscious he brought about sudden vicissitudes which, by a chain of logical sequences, would produce, at specific points in his dream, the person required to receive his love or to startle him awake. In an instant night grew black about him; a tocsin sounded, people ran past him, escaping from their blazing houses; he could hear the thunder of the surging waves, and also of his own heart, which with equal violence was anxiously beating in his breast. Suddenly the speed of these palpitations redoubled, he felt an inexplicable pain and nausea. A peasant, dreadfully burned, flung at him as he passed: "Come and ask Charlus where Odette spent the night with her friend. He used to go about with her in the past, and she tells him everything. It was they who started the fire." It was his valet, come to awaken him, and saying:—

"Sir, it's eight o'clock, and the barber is here. I've told him to call again in an hour."

But these words, as they plunged through the waves of sleep in which Swann was submerged, did not reach his consciousness without undergoing that refraction which turns a ray of light in the depths of water into another sun; just as, a moment earlier, the sound of the door-bell, swelling in the depths of his abyss of sleep into the clangour of a tocsin, had engendered the episode of the fire. Meanwhile, the scenery of his dream-stage scattered into dust, he opened his eyes, and heard for the last time the boom of a wave in the sea, now distant. He touched his cheek. It was dry. And yet he remembered the sting of the cold spray, and the taste of salt on his lips. He rose and dressed himself. He had made the barber come early because he had written the day before to my grandfather to say that he was going to Combray that afternoon, having learned that Mme de Cambremer—Mlle Legrandin that had been—was spending a few days there. The association in his memory of her young and charming face with a countryside he had not visited for so long offered him a combined attraction which had made him decide at last to leave Paris for a while. As the different circumstances that bring us into contact with certain people do not coincide with the period in which we are in love with them, but, overlapping it, may occur before love has begun, and may be repeated after it has ended, the earliest appearances in our lives of a person who is destined to take our fancy later on assume retrospectively in our eyes a certain value as an indication, a warning, a presage. It was in this fashion that Swann had often reverted in his mind to the image of Odette

encountered in the theatre on that first evening when he had
no thought of ever seeing her again—and that he now
recalled the party at Mme de Saint-Euverte's at which he had
introduced General de Froberville to Mme de Cambremer.
So manifold are our interests in life that it is not uncommon,
on the self-same occasion, for the foundations of a happiness
which does not yet exist to be laid down simultaneously with
the aggravation of a grief from which we are still suffering.
And doubtless this could have occurred to Swann elsewhere
than at Mme de Saint-Euverte's. Who indeed can say whether,
in the event of his having gone elsewhere that evening, other
happinesses, other griefs might not have come to him, which
later would have appeared to him to have been inevitable?
But what did seem to him to have been inevitable was what
had indeed taken place, and he was not far short of seeing
something providential in the fact that he had decided to go
to Mme de Saint-Euverte's that evening, because his mind,
anxious to admire the richness of invention that life shows,
and incapable of facing a difficult problem for any length of
time, such as deciding what was most to be wished for, came
to the conclusion that the sufferings through which he had
passed that evening, and the pleasures, as yet unsuspected,
which were already germinating there—the exact balance
between which was too difficult to establish—were linked by
a sort of concatenation of necessity.

But while, an hour after his awakening, he was giving

instructions to the barber to see that his stiffly brushed hair should not become disarranged on the journey, he thought of his dream again, and saw once again, as he had felt them close beside him, Odette's pallid complexion, her too thin cheeks, her drawn features, her tired eyes, all the things which—in the course of those successive bursts of affection which had made of his enduring love for Odette a long oblivion of the first impression that he had formed of her—he had ceased to notice since the early days of their intimacy, days to which doubtless, while he slept, his memory had returned to seek their exact sensation. And with the old, intermittent caddishness which reappeared in him when he was no longer unhappy and his moral standards dropped accordingly, he exclaimed to himself: "To think that I've wasted years of my life, that I've longed to die, that I've experienced my greatest love, for a woman who didn't appeal to me, who wasn't even my type!"

$\mathcal{MID\text{-}AUTUMN}$

ROBERT OLEN BUTLER

*Learning to love again does not mean you must forget
the past. The Vietnamese narrator of this sad and
beautiful sketch by National Book Award winner
Robert Olen Butler is living in the United States,
married to an American, and expecting a child.
But the feelings she still has for her Vietnamese
fiancé, Bao, who was killed in the war,
prove that new love can grow
amid a jungle of memories.*

We are lucky, you and I, to be Vietnamese so that I can speak to you even before you are born. This is why I use the Vietnamese language. It is our custom for the mother to begin this conversation with the child in the womb, to begin counseling you in matters of the world that you will soon enter. It is not a custom among the Americans, so perhaps you would not even understand English if I spoke it. Nor could I speak in English nearly so well, to tell you some of the things of my heart. Above all you must listen to my heart. The language is not important. I don't know if you can hear all the other words, the ones in English that float about us like the pollen that in the spring makes me sneeze and that lets the flowers bear their own children. I think I remember from our country that this is a private conversation, that it is only my voice that you can hear, but I do not know for sure. My mother is dead now and cannot answer this question. She spoke to me when I was in her womb and sometimes, when I dream and wake and cannot remember, I have the feeling that the dream was of her voice plunging like a naked swimmer into that sea and swimming strongly to me, who waited deep beneath the waves.

And when you move inside me, my little one, when you try to swim higher, coming up to meet me, I look at the two oaken barrels I have filled with red blooms, the hibiscus.

They have no smell to speak of, but they are very pretty, and sometimes the hummingbirds come with their invisible wings and with their little bodies as slick as if they had just flown up from the sea. I look also at the white picket fence, very white without any stain of mildew, though the air is warm here in Louisiana all the time, and very wet. And sometimes, like at this moment, I look beyond this yard, lifting my eyes above the ragged line of trees to the sky. It is a sky that looks like the skies in Vietnam. Sometimes full of tiny blooms of clouds as still as flowers floating on a bowl in the center of a New Year's table. Sometimes full of great dark bodies, Chinese warriors rolling their shoulders, huffing up with a summer storm that we know will pass. One day you will run out into the storm, laughing, like all the children of Vietnam.

I saw you for the first time last week. The doctor spread a jelly on my stomach and it was the coldest thing I have ever felt, even more cold than the snow I once held melting in my hands. He ran a microphone up and down my stomach and I saw you on a screen, the shape of you. I could see inside you. I could see your spine and I could see your heart beating and this is what reminded me of my duty to you. And my joy. To speak. And he told me you were a girl.

Please understand that I love you, that you are a girl. My own mother never knew my sex as she spoke to me. And I know that she was a Vietnamese mother and so she must have been disappointed when she came to find out that I was a girl, when she held me for the first time and she shared the cast-down look of my father that I was not a son for them. This is the way in Vietnam. I know that the words she spoke to me in the womb were as a boy; she was hoping that I was a boy and not ever bringing the bad luck on themselves by acting as if I was anything else but a son. But, little one, I am glad you are a girl. You will understand me even better.

A marriage in Vietnam is a strange and wonderful thing. There is a genie of marriage. We call him the Rose Silk Thread God, though he is not quite a god. I can say this because I am already married, but if I was single and living once more in the village where I grew up in Vietnam, I would call him a god and do all the right things to make him smile on me. A special altar is made and we light candles and incense in honor of this genie. There is a ceremony on the day of marriage led by the male head of the groom's family, and everyone bows before the altar and prays, and a plea to the genie for his protection and help is written on a piece of rose-colored silk paper and then read aloud. A cup is filled with wine and the head of the groom's family sips from it and gives it to the groom, who sips from it and gives it to his bride. She drinks, and I am told that this is the most delicious thing that she will ever taste. I do not know who told me this. Perhaps my mother. Perhaps I learned it when I was in her womb. Then after the bride has drunk the wine that has touched the lips of the men, the sheet of silk paper is burned.

The flame is pale rose, and the threads of silk rise in the heat before they vanish.

My little one, I was once very young. I was sixteen and I was very beautiful and I met Bao when he was seventeen. It was at the most wonderful time of year for lovers to meet, at the Mid-Autumn Festival. I saw him in the morning as I was coming up the footpath from the cistern. My hands and my face and my arms up nearly to my shoulders were slick and cool from my plunging them into the water of the cistern. The cistern held the drinking water for my hamlet, but no one had been looking and I knew I was clean because I had bathed that morning in the river and the water had looked so still and fine that I could not resist plunging my arms in and my face. When I came up out of the water, the sun that had been harsh with me all morning was suddenly my friend, tugging gently at my skin and making me feel very calm.

I filled my family's jug and started up the path, and when I encountered this tall boy coming down the path with a strong step, my first thought was that he was coming to catch me and punish me for touching the water that the hamlet must drink. I looked at his face and his eyes were so very black and they seized on my face with such a fervor that I almost dropped the jug. I thought it was fear that I felt, but later I knew it had not been fear.

He lunged forward and caught the jug of water and it splashed him on the face and the chest and he laughed. When he laughed, I grew weaker still and he had to take the jug onto his own shoulder and turn and walk with me up the path to my house. We did not say many words. We laughed several times in silent recollection of the falling jug and the splashing water. And we looked at each other with side glances as we walked. Sometimes I would look and he would not be looking; sometimes I knew he was looking and I did not look; but other times one of us would look and the other would be looking at just the same time and we would laugh again. At last my legs grew heavy, though, as we neared my house. I told him we now had to part, and as he slowly took the jug of water from his shoulder and gave it to me, he said that his name was Bao and he was from a different hamlet but he was staying here for a time with a cousin and he asked if I would be out celebrating the moon tonight and I said yes.

The Mid-Autumn Festival is all about the moon, my little one. It is held on the fifteenth day of the eighth lunar month, when there is the brightest moon of the year. The Chinese gave us the celebration because one of their early emperors loved poetry and he wrote many poems himself. Since all poets are full of silver threads that rise inside them as the moon grows large, the emperor yearned to go to the moon. On the fifteenth day of the eighth lunar month this yearning grew unbearable, and he called his wizard to him and told him he must find a way. So the wizard worked hard, chanting spells and burning special incense, and finally in a blinding flash of light the wizard fell to the ground, and there in the palace courtyard was the root of a great rainbow which arched up into the night sky and went all the way to the moon.

The emperor saddled his best horse and armed himself with a sheaf of his own poems and he spurred the horse onto the rainbow and he galloped off to the moon. When he got there, he found a beautiful island in the middle of a great, dark sea. On the island he dismounted his horse and he was surrounded by fairies who lifted him up and danced and sang their poems and he sang his and it was the most wonderful time of his fife, borne on the shoulders of these lovely creatures and feeling as if he belonged there, his deepest self belonged in this place, so full of wonder it was. But he could not stay. His people needed him. There was another world to deal with. So with great reluctance he got onto his horse and rode back down to his palace.

The next morning the rainbow was gone. The emperor did all the things he needed to do for his people and one night he thought that he had earned a rest, that he could return to the moon at least until morning. But the wizard came at his call and sadly explained that there was no return to the moon. Once you came down the rainbow, there was no way back. The emperor was very sad, so he proclaimed that every year on the fifteenth night of the eighth lunar month, the anniversary of his trip, there would be a celebration throughout the kingdom to remember the beautiful land that was left behind.

My little one, you would love all the paper lanterns that we light on this night. They are in the shapes of dragons and unicorns and stars and boats and horses and hares and toads. We light candles inside them and we swing them on sticks in the dark and the village is full of these wonderful pinwheels of light, the rushing of these bright shapes. I saw Bao again in such a light, with the swirling of lanterns and the moon just coming over the horizon, fat as an elephant and the color of the sun in fog. I saw him in the center of the hamlet where we had all gathered to celebrate and the lights were whirling and when our eyes met, he suddenly staggered under the weight of an invisible water jug, he carried it around and around in circles on his shoulder, a wonderful pantomime, and then he lost his footing and I could almost see the jug there on his shoulder tipping, tipping, and it fell and crashed and he jumped back from all the splashing water and we laughed.

At the festival of the moon, it is not forbidden for an unbetrothed boy and girl to speak together. We moved toward each other and I could feel the heat of the swinging lanterns on my face as the children ran near me and cut in before me, but Bao and I kept moving and we came together in the center of the village square and we spoke. He asked if my family was well and I asked about his family and I was happy to find that the father of his cousin was a good friend of my father. Bao asked if my water jug was safe and I asked if his shoulder was in pain from carrying the jug and we slowly edged our way to the darkness beyond the celebrating and then we walked down the path to the cistern and beyond, to the edge of the river.

This was perhaps more than our hamlet's customs would allow us, but we did not think of that. I was a strong-headed girl, my little one, and Bao was a good boy. I sensed that of him and I was right. He was very respectful to me. I felt very safe. We stood by the river and a sampan slipped silently past and it was hung with orange lanterns, the color of the moon from earlier this night, when it was near the horizon and Bao did his pantomime for me.

Now the moon was higher and it had grown slimmer and it had turned so white that it nearly hurt my eyes to look at it. Nearly hurt them but not quite, and so it was the most beautiful of all. It was as bright as it could be and still be a good thing. And Bao slipped his arm around my waist and I let him keep it there and the joy of it was as strong as it could be and still be a good thing. We stood looking up at the moon and trying to see the fairies there in the middle of the dark sea and we tried to hear them singing their poems.

My little one, Bao was my love and both our families loved us, too, so much so that they agreed to let us marry. In Vietnam this was a very rare thing, that the marriage agreement should be the same as the agreement of hearts between the bride and the groom. You will be lucky, too. This is a good thing about being in America. A very good thing, and I wonder if you can tell that there are tears in my eyes now, if you can sense this little fall of water, surrounded as you are by your own sea. But do not worry. These tears are happy ones, tears for you and the life you will have, which will be very beautiful.

I look at the gate in our white picket fence and soon your father will come through. I want to tell you that you are a lucky girl. Even as my tears change. Bao and I were betrothed to be married. And then he was called into the Army and he went away before the ceremony could be arranged and he died in a battle somewhere in the mountains. The gate is opening now and your father, my husband, is coming through and he is a good man. He keeps this fence and our house free from the mildew. He scrubs it with bleach and hoses it every six months and he stops at my hibiscus, not seeing me here at the window. I must soon stop speaking. He is a good man, an American soldier who loved his Vietnamese woman for true and for always. He will find me by the window and touch my cheek gently with the back of his fine, strong hand and he will touch my belly, trying to think he is touching you.

You will love him, my little one, and since I know you

understand my heart, I do not want you to be sad for me. I had my night on the moon and when I came back down the rainbow, the world I found was also good. It is sad that there is no return, but we can still light a lantern and look into the night sky and remember.

from

THE ACCIDENTAL TOURIST

ANNE TYLER

When Macon and Sarah Leary lose their son Ethan,
the decay of their relationship becomes glaringly
apparent in the light of grief. Although Macon tries a
new relationship with Muriel—with her red talon
nails and passion for thrift shops—he still can't
let go of Sarah. But Muriel follows him on a
writing assignment to Paris . . .
where fate takes over.

She said at the end of the evening that she wished he would come to her room—couldn't he? to guard against bad dreams?—and he said no and told her good night. And then he felt how she drew at him, pulling deep strings from inside him, when the elevator creaked away with her.

In his sleep he conceived a plan to take her along tomorrow. What harm would it do? It was only a day trip. Over and over in his scattered, fitful sleep he picked up his phone and dialed her room. It was a surprise, when he woke in the morning, to find he hadn't invited her yet.

He sat up and reached for the phone and remembered only then—with the numb receiver pressed to his ear—that the phone was out of order and he'd forgotten to report it. He wondered if it were something he could repair himself, a cord unplugged or something. He rose and peered behind the bureau. He stooped to hunt for a jack of some kind.

And his back went out.

No doubt about it—that little twang! in a muscle to the left of his spine. The pain was so sharp it snagged his breath. Then it faded. Maybe it was gone for good. He straightened, a minimal movement. But it was enough to bring the pain zinging in again.

He lowered himself to the bed inch by inch. The hard part was getting his feet up, but he set his face and accomplished that too. Then he lay pondering what to do next.

Once he had had this happen and the pain had vanished in five minutes and not returned it. It had been only a freaky thing like a foot cramp.

But then, once he'd stayed flat in bed for two weeks and crept around like a very old man for another month after that.

He lay rearranging his agenda in his mind. If he canceled one trip, postponed another . . . Yes, possibly what he'd planned for the next three days could be squeezed into two instead, if only he were able to get around by tomorrow.

He must have gone back to sleep. He didn't know for how long. He woke to a knock and thought it was breakfast, though he'd left instructions for none to be brought today. But then he heard Muriel. "Macon? You in there?" She was hoping he hadn't left Paris yet; she was here to beg again to go with him. He knew that as clearly as if she'd announced it. He was grateful now for the spasm that gripped him as he turned away from her voice. Somehow that short sleep had cleared his head, and he saw that he'd come perilously close to falling in with her again. *Falling in*: That was the way he put it to himself. What luck that his back had stopped him. Another minute—another few seconds—and he might have been lost.

He dropped into sleep so suddenly that he didn't even hear her walk away.

When he woke again it was much later, he felt, although he didn't want to go through the contortions necessary to look at his watch. A wheeled cart was passing his room and he heard voices—hotel employees, probably—laughing in the corridor. They must be so comfortable here; they must all know each other so well. There was a knock on his door, then a jingle of keys. A small, pale chambermaid poked her face in and said, *"Pardon, monsieur."* She started to retreat but then stopped and asked him something in French, and he gestured toward his back and winced. "Ah," she said, entering, and she said something else very rapidly. (She would be telling him about *her* back.) He said, "If you could just help me up, please," for he had decided he had no choice but to go call Julian. She seemed to understand what he meant and came over to the bed. He turned onto his stomach and then struggled up on one arm—the only way he could manage to rise without excruciating pain. The chambermaid took his other arm and braced herself beneath his weight as he stood. She was much shorter than he, and pretty in a fragile, meek way. He was conscious of his unshaven face and his rumpled pajamas. "My jacket," he told her, and they proceeded haltingly to the chair where his suit jacket hung. She draped it around his shoulders. Then he said, "Downstairs? To the telephone?" She looked over at the phone on the bureau, but he made a negative movement with the flat of his hand—a gesture that cost him. He grimaced. She clucked her tongue and led him out into the corridor.

Walking was not particularly difficult; he felt hardly a

twinge. But the elevator jerked agonizingly and there was no way he could predict it. The chambermaid uttered soft sounds of sympathy. When they arrived in the lobby she led him to the telephone booth and started to seat him, but he said, "No, no, standing's easier. Thanks." She backed out and left him there. He saw her talking to the clerk at the desk, shaking her head in pity; the clerk shook his head, too.

Macon worried Julian wouldn't be in his office yet, and he didn't know his home number. But the phone was answered on the very first ring. "Businessman's Press." A woman's voice, confusingly familiar, threading beneath the hiss of long distance.

"Um—" he said. "This is Macon Leary. To whom am I—"

"Oh, Macon."

"Rose?"

"Yes, it's me."

"What are *you* doing there?"

"I work here now."

"Oh, I see."

"I'm putting things in order. You wouldn't believe the state this place is in."

"Rose, my back has gone out on me," Macon said.

"Oh, no, of all times! Are you still in Paris?"

"Yes, but I was just about to start my day trips and there are all these plans I have to change—appointments, travel reservations—and no telephone in my room. So I was wondering if Julian could do it from his end. Maybe he could get the reservations from Becky and—"

"I'll take care of it myself," Rose said. "Don't you bother with a thing."

"I don't know when I'm going to get to the other cities, tell him. I don't have any idea when I'll be—"

"We'll work it out. Have you seen a doctor?"

"Doctors don't help. Just bed rest."

"Well, rest then, Macon."

He gave her the name of his hotel, and she repeated it briskly and then told him to get on back to bed.

When he emerged from the phone booth the chamber-maid had a bellboy there to help him, and between the two of them he made it to his room without much trouble. They were very solicitous. They seemed anxious about leaving him alone, but he assured them he would be all right.

All that afternoon he lay in bed, rising twice to go to the bathroom and once to get some milk from the mini-bar. He wasn't really hungry. He watched the brown flowers on the wall-paper; he thought he had never known a hotel room so inti-mately. The side of the bureau next to the bed had a streak in the woodgrain that looked like a bony man in a hat.

At suppertime he took a small bottle of wine from the mini-bar and inched himself into the armchair to drink it. Even the motion of raising the bottle to his lips caused him pain, but he thought the wine would help him sleep. While he was sitting there the chambermaid knocked and let herself in. She asked him, evidently, whether he wanted anything to eat, but he thanked her and said no. She must have been on her way home; she carried a battered little pocketbook.

Later there was another knock, after he had dragged himself back to bed, and Muriel said, "Macon? Macon?" He kept absolutely silent. She went away.

The air grew fuzzy and then dark. The man on the side of the bureau faded. Footsteps crossed the floor above him.

He had often wondered how many people died in hotels. The law of averages said some would, right? And some who had no close relatives—say one of his readers, a salesman without a family—well, what was done about such people? Was there some kind of potters' field for unknown travelers?

He could lie in only two positions—on his left side or on his back—and switching from one to the other meant waking up, consciously deciding to undertake the ordeal, plotting his strategy. Then he returned to a fretful semiconsciousness.

He dreamed he was seated on an airplane next to a woman dressed all in gray, a very narrow, starched, thin-lipped woman, and he tried to hold perfectly still because he sensed she disapproved of movement. It was a rule of hers; he knew that somehow. But he grew more and more uncomfortable, and so he decided to confront her. He said, "Ma'am?" She turned her eyes on him, mild, mournful eyes under finely arched brows. "Miss MacIntosh!" he said. He woke in a spasm of pain. He felt as if a tiny, cruel hand had snatched up part of his back and wrung it out.

When the waiter brought his breakfast in the morning, the chambermaid came along. She must keep grueling hours, Macon thought. But he was glad to see her. She and the waiter fussed over him, mixing his hot milk and coffee, and the waiter helped him into the bathroom while the chambermaid changed his sheets. He thanked them over and over; *"Merci,"* he said, clumsily. He wished he knew the French for, "I don't know why you're being so kind." After they left he ate all of his rolls, which the chambermaid had thoughtfully buttered and spread with strawberry jam. Then he turned on the TV for company and got back in bed.

He was sorry about the TV when he heard the knock on the door, because he thought it was Muriel and she would hear. But it seemed early for Muriel to be awake. And then a key turned in the lock, and in walked Sarah.

He said, "Sarah?"

She wore a beige suit, and she carried two pieces of matched luggage, and she brought a kind of breeze of efficiency with her. "Now, everything's taken care of," she told him. "I'm going to make your day trips for you." She set down her suitcases, kissed his forehead, and picked up a glass from his breakfast table. As she went off to the bathroom she said, "We've rescheduled the other cities and I start on them tomorrow."

"But how did you get here so soon?" he asked.

She came out of the bathroom; the glass was full of water. "You have Rose to thank for that," she said, switching off the TV. "Rose is just a wizard. She's revamped that entire office. Here's a pill from Dr. Levitt."

"You know I don't take pills," he said.

"This time you do," she told him. She helped him rise up on one elbow. "You're going to sleep as much as you can, so your back has a chance to heal. Swallow."

The pill was tiny and very bitter. He could taste it even after he'd lain down again.

"Is the pain bad?" she asked him.

"Kind of."

"How've you been getting your meals?"

"Well, breakfast comes anyway, of course. That's about it."

"I'll ask about room service," she told him, picking up the phone. "Since I'll be gone so . . . What's the matter with the telephone?"

"It's dead."

"I'll go tell the desk. Can I bring you anything while I'm out?"

"No, thank you."

When she left, he almost wondered if he'd imagined her. Except that her suitcases sat next to his bed, sleek and creamy—the same ones she kept on the closet shelf at home.

He thought about Muriel, about what would happen if

she were to knock now. Then he thought about two nights ago, or was it three, when she had strolled in with all her purchases. He wondered if she'd left any traces. A belt lost under the bed, a glass disk fallen off her cocktail dress? He began to worry about it seriously. It seemed to him almost inevitable; of course she'd left something. The only question was, what. And where.

Groaning, he rolled over and pushed himself upright. He struggled off the bed and then sagged to his knees to peer beneath it. There didn't seem to be anything there. He got to his feet and tilted over the armchair to feel around the edges of the cushion. Nothing there either. Actually she hadn't gone anywhere near the armchair, to his recollection; nor had she gone to the bureau, but even so he slid out the drawers one by one to make sure. His own belongings—just a handful—occupied one drawer. The others were empty, but the second one down had a sprinkling of pink face powder. It wasn't Muriel's, of course, but it looked like hers. He decided to get rid of it. He tottered into the bathroom, dampened a towel, and came back to swab the drawer clean. Then he saw that the towel had developed a large pink smear, as if a woman wearing too much makeup had wiped her face with it. He folded the towel so the smear was concealed and laid it in the back of the drawer. No, too incriminating. He took it out again and hid it beneath the armchair cushion. That didn't seem right either. Finally he went into the bathroom and washed the towel by hand, scrubbing it with a bar of soap till the spot was completely gone. The pain in his back was constant, and beads of sweat stood out on his forehead. At some point he decided he was acting very peculiar; in fact it must be the pill; and he dropped the wet towel in a heap on the floor and crawled back into bed. He fell asleep at once. It wasn't a normal sleep; it was a kind of burial.

He knew Sarah came in but he couldn't wake up to greet her. And he knew she left again. He heard someone knock, he heard lunch being brought, he heard the chambermaid whisper, *"Monsieur?"* He remained in his stupor. The pain was muffled but still present—just covered up, he thought; the pill worked like those inferior room sprays in advertisements, the ones that only mask offending odors. Then Sarah came back for the second time and he opened his eyes. She was standing over the bed with a glass of water. "How do you feel?" she asked him.

"Okay," he said.

"Here's your next pill."

"Sarah, those things are deadly."

"They help, don't they?"

"They knock me out," he said. But he took the pill.

She sat down on the edge of the mattress, careful not to jar him. She still wore her suit and looked freshly groomed, although she must be bushed by now. "Macon," she said quietly.

"Hmm."

"I saw that woman friend of yours."

He tensed. His back seized up.

"She saw me, too," she said. "She seemed very surprised."

"Sarah, this is not the way it looks," he told her.

"What is it then, Macon? I'd like to hear."

"She came over on her own. I didn't even know till just before the plane took off, I swear it! She followed me. I told her I didn't want her along. I told her it was no use."

She kept looking at him. "You didn't know till just before the plane took off," she said.

"I swear it," he said.

He wished he hadn't taken the pill. He felt he wasn't in full possession of his faculties.

"Do you believe me?" he asked her.

"Yes, I believe you," she said, and then she got up and started uncovering his lunch dishes.

He spent the afternoon in another stupor, but he was aware of the chambermaid's checking on him twice, and he was almost fully awake when Sarah came in with a bag of groceries. "I thought I'd make you supper myself," she told him. "Fresh fruit and things; you always complain you don't get enough fresh fruit when you travel."

"That's very nice of you, Sarah."

He worked himself around till he was half sitting, propped against a pillow. Sarah was unwrapping cheeses. "The phone's fixed," she said. "You'll be able to call for your meals and all while I'm out. Then I was thinking: After I've finished the trips, if your back is better, maybe we could do a little sight-seeing on our own. Take some time for ourselves, since we're here. Visit a few museums and such."

"Fine," he said.

"Have a second honeymoon, sort of."

"Wonderful."

He watched her set the cheeses on a flattened paper bag. "We'll change your plane ticket for a later date," she said. "You're reserved to leave tomorrow morning; no chance you could manage that. I left my own ticket open-ended. Julian said I should. Did I tell you where Julian is living?"

"No, where?"

"He's moved in with Rose and your brothers."

"He's what?"

"I took Edward over to Rose's to stay while I was gone, and there was Julian. He sleeps in Rose's bedroom; he's started playing Vaccination every night after supper."

"Well, I'll be damned," Macon said.

"Have some cheese."

He accepted a slice, changing position as little as possible.

"Funny, sometimes Rose reminds me of a flounder," Sarah said. "Not in looks, of course . . . She's lain on the ocean floor so long, one eye has moved to the other side of her head."

He stopped chewing and stared at her. She was pouring two glasses of cloudy brown liquid. "Apple cider," she told him. "I figured you shouldn't drink wine with those pills."

"Oh. Right," he said.

She passed him a glass. "A toast to our second honeymoon," she said.

"Our second honeymoon," he echoed.

"Twenty-one more years together."

"Twenty-one!" he said. It sounded like such a lot.

"Or would you say twenty."

"No, it's twenty-one, all right. We were married in nineteen—"

"I mean because we skipped this past year."

"Oh," he said. "No, it would still be twenty-one."

"You think so?"

"I consider last year just another stage in our marriage," he said. "Don't worry: It's twenty-one."

She clinked her glass against his.

Their main dish was a potted meat that she spread on French bread, and their dessert was fruit. She washed the fruit in the bathroom, returning with handfuls of peaches and strawberries; and meanwhile she kept up a cozy patter that made him feel he was home again. "Did I mention we had a letter from the Averys? They might be passing through Baltimore later this summer. Oh, and the termite man came."

"Ah."

"He couldn't find anything wrong, he said."

"Well, that's a relief."

"And I've almost finished my sculpture and Mr. Armistead says it's the best thing I've done."

"Good for you," Macon said.

"Oh," she said, folding the last paper bag, "I know you don't think my sculptures are important, but—"

"Who says I don't?" he asked.

"I know you think I'm just this middle-aged lady playing artist—"

"Who says?"

"Oh, I know what you think! You don't have to pretend with me."

Macon started to slump against his pillow, but was brought up short by a muscle spasm.

She cut a peach into sections, and then she sat on the bed and passed him one of the sections. She said, "Macon. Just tell me this. Was the little boy the attraction?"

"Huh?"

"Was the fact that she had a child what attracted you to that woman?"

He said, "Sarah, I swear to you, I had no idea she was planning to follow me over here."

"Yes, I realize that," she said, "but I was wondering about the child question."

"What child question?"

"I was remembering the time you said we should have another baby."

"Oh, well, that was just . . . I don't know what that was," he said. He handed her back the peach; he wasn't hungry anymore.

"I was thinking maybe you were right," Sarah said.

"What? No, Sarah; Lord, that was a terrible idea."

"Oh, I know it's scary," she told him. "I admit I'd be scared to have another."

"Exactly," Macon said. "We're too old."

"No, I'm talking about the, you know, world we'd be bringing him into. So much evil and danger. I admit it: I'd be frantic any time we let him out on the street."

Macon saw Singleton Street in his mind, small and distant like Julian's little green map of Hawaii and full of gaily drawn people scrubbing their stoops, tinkering with their cars, splashing under fire hydrants.

"Oh, well, you're right," he said. "Though really it's kind of . . . heartening, isn't it? How most human beings do try. How they try to be as responsible and kind as they can manage."

"Are you saying yes, we can have a baby?" Sarah asked.

Macon swallowed. He said, "Well, no. It seems to me we're past the time for that, Sarah."

"So," she said, "her little boy wasn't the reason."

"Look, it's over with. Can't we close the lid on it? I don't cross-examine *you*, do I?"

"But I don't have someone following me to Paris!" she said.

"And what if you did? Do you think I'd hold you to blame if someone just climbed on a plane without your knowing?"

"Before it left the ground," she said.

"Pardon? Well, I should hope so!"

"Before it left the ground, you saw her. You could have walked up to her and said, 'No. Get off. Go this minute. I want nothing more to do with you and I never want to see you again.'"

"You think I own the airline, Sarah?"

"You could have stopped her if you'd really wanted," Sarah said. "You could have taken steps."

And then she rose and began to clear away their supper.

She gave him his next pill, but he let it stay in his fist a while because he didn't want to risk moving. He lay with his eyes closed, listening to Sarah undress. She ran water in the bathroom, slipped the chain on the door, turned off the lights. When she got into bed it stabbed his back, even though she settled carefully, but he gave no sign. He heard her breathing soften almost at once. She must have been exhausted.

He reflected that he had not taken steps very often in his life, come to think of it. Really never. His marriage, his two jobs, his time with Muriel, his return to Sarah—all seemed to have simply befallen him. He couldn't think of a single major act he had managed of his own accord.

Was it too late now to begin?

Was there any way he could learn to do things differently?

He opened his hand and let the pill fall among the bed-clothes. It was going to be a restless, uncomfortable night, but anything was better than floating off on that stupor again.

In the morning, he negotiated the journey out of bed and into the bathroom. He shaved and dressed, spending long minutes on each task. Creeping around laboriously, he packed his bag. The heaviest thing he packed was *Miss MacIntosh, My Darling*, and after thinking that over a while, he took it out again and set it on the bureau.

Sarah said, "Macon?"

"Sarah. I'm glad you're awake," he said.

"What are you doing?"

"I'm packing to leave."

She sat up. Her face was creased down one side.

"But what about your back?" she asked. "And I've got all those appointments! And we were going to take a second honeymoon!"

"Sweetheart," he said. He lowered himself cautiously till he was sitting on the bed. He picked up her hand. It stayed lifeless while she watched his face.

"You're going back to that woman," she said.

"Yes, I am," he said.

"Why, Macon?"

"I just decided, Sarah. I thought about it most of last night. It wasn't easy. It's not the easy way out, believe me."

She sat staring at him. She wore no expression.

"Well, I don't want to miss the plane," he said.

He inched to a standing position and hobbled into the bathroom for his shaving kit.

"You know what this is? It's all due to that pill!" Sarah called after him. "You said yourself it knocks you out!"

"I didn't take the pill."

There was a silence.

She said, "Macon? Are you just trying to get even with me for the time I left you?"

He returned with the shaving kit and said, "No, sweetheart."

"I suppose you realize what your life is going to be like," she said. She climbed out of bed. She stood next to him in her nightgown, hugging her bare arms. "You'll be one of those mismatched couples no one invites to parties. No one will know what to make of you. People will wonder whenever they meet you, 'My God, what does he see in her? Why choose someone so inappropriate? It's grotesque, how does he put up with her?' And her friends will no doubt be asking the same about you."

"That's probably true," Macon said. He felt a mild stirring of interest; he saw now how such couples evolved. They were not, as he'd always supposed, the result of some ludicrous lack of perception, but had come together for reasons that the rest of the world would never guess.

He zipped his overnight bag.

"I'm sorry, Sarah. I didn't want to decide this," he said.

He put his arm around her painfully, and after a pause she let her head rest against his shoulder. It struck him that even this moment was just another stage in their marriage. There would probably be still other stages in their thirtieth year, fortieth year—forever, no matter what separate paths they chose to travel.

He didn't take the elevator; he felt he couldn't bear the willy-nilliness of it. He went down the stairs instead. He managed the front door by backing through it, stiffly.

Out on the street he found the usual bustle of a weekday morning—shopgirls hurrying past, men with briefcases. No taxis in sight. He set off for the next block, where his chances were better. Walking was fairly easy but carrying his bag was torture. Lightweight though it was, it twisted his back out of line. He tried it in his left hand, then his right. And after all, what was inside it? Pajamas, a change of underwear, emergency supplies he never used . . . He stepped over to a building, a bank or office building with a low stone curb running around its base. He set the bag on the curb and hurried on.

Up ahead he saw a taxi with a boy just stepping out of it,

but he discovered too late that hailing it was going to be a problem. Raising either arm was impossible. So he was forced to run in an absurd, scuttling fashion while shouting bits of French he'd never said aloud before: *"Attendez! Attendez, monsieur!"*

The taxi was already moving off and the boy was just slipping his wallet back into his jeans, but then he looked up and saw Macon. He acted fast; he spun and called out something and the taxi braked. *"Merci beaucoup,"* Macon panted, and the boy, who had a sweet, pure face and shaggy yellow hair, opened the taxi door for him and gently assisted him in. "Oof!" Macon said, seized by a spasm. The boy shut the door and then, to Macon's surprise, lifted a hand in a formal goodbye. The taxi moved off. Macon told the driver where he was going and sank back into his seat. He patted his inside pocket, checking passport, plane ticket. He unfolded his handkerchief and wiped his forehead.

Evidently his sense of direction had failed him, as usual. The driver was making a U-turn, heading back where Macon had just come from. They passed the boy once again. He had a jaunty, stiff-legged way of walking that seemed familiar.

If Ethan hadn't died, Macon thought, wouldn't he have grown into such a person?

He would have turned to give the boy another look, except that he couldn't manage the movement.

The taxi bounced over the cobblestones. The driver

whistled a tune between his teeth. Macon found that bracing himself on one arm protected his back somewhat from the jolts. Every now and then, though, a pothole caught him off guard.

And if dead people aged, wouldn't it be a comfort? To think of Ethan growing up in heaven—fourteen years old now instead of twelve—eased the grief a little. Oh, it was their immunity to time that made the dead so heartbreaking. (Look at the husband who dies young, the wife aging on without him; how sad to imagine the husband coming back to find her so changed.) Macon gazed out the cab window, considering the notion in his mind. He felt a kind of inner rush, a racing forward. The real adventure, he thought, is the flow of time; it's as much adventure as anyone could wish. And if he pictured Ethan still part of that flow—in some other place, however unreachable—he believed he might be able to bear it after all.

The taxi passed Macon's hotel—brown and tidy, strangely homelike. A man was just emerging with a small anxious dog on his arm. And there on the curb stood Muriel, surrounded by suitcases and string-handled shopping bags and cardboard cartons overflowing with red velvet. She was frantically waving down taxis—first one ahead, then Macon's own. *"Arrêtez!"* Macon cried to the driver. The taxi lurched to a halt. A sudden flash of sunlight hit the windshield, and spangles flew across the glass. The spangles were old water spots, or maybe the markings of leaves, but for a moment Macon thought they were something else. They were so bright and festive, for a moment he thought they were confetti.

from

THE VAGABOND

COLETTE

After eight years of unhappy marriage to a cruel,
adulterous man followed by a painful, shameful
divorce, Renée is on her own. It takes a new suitor's
persistent, patient pursuit and a "long, drowsy
kiss" to remind her that love is not
entirely lost for her.

Heavens, how tired I am, absolutely worn out! I fell asleep after lunch, as I sometimes do on rehearsal days, and I've wakened up utterly weary, feeling as though I had come from the ends of the earth, astonished and sad and barely able to think, eyeing my familiar furniture with a hostile gaze. Just such an awakening, in fact, as the most horrible of those I used to experience in the days of my suffering. But since I am not suffering now, what can the reason be?

I feel unable to move. I look at my hand hanging down as though it did not belong to me. I don't recognize the stuff of my frock. Who was it, while I slept, who loosened the coronet of plaits coiled about my brows like the tresses of a grave young Ceres? I was . . . I was . . . there was a garden . . . a peach-coloured sunset sky . . . a shrill childish voice answering the cries of the swallows . . . yes, and that sound like distant water, sometimes powerful and sometimes muffled: the breath of a forest. I had gone back to the beginning of my life. What a journey to catch up with myself again, where I am now! I cry for the sleep that has fled, the dark curtain which sheltered me and now has withdrawn itself, leaving me shivering and naked. Sick people who think they are cured experience these fresh attacks of their malady which find them childishly astonished and plaintive: 'But I thought it was over!' For two pins I could groan aloud, as they do.

O dangerous and too-kindly sleep which in less than an hour obliterates the memory of myself! Whence come I, and on what wings, that it should take me so long, humiliated and exiled, to accept that I am myself? Renée Néré, dancer and mime ... Was my proud childhood, my withdrawn and passionate adolescence, which welcomed love so fearlessly, to lead to no end but that?

O Margot, my discouraging friend, if only I had strength to get up, and run to you, and tell you ... But my courage is the only thing you admire and I should not dare to falter before you. I feel pretty sure that your virile gaze and the clasp of your dry little hand, chapped by cold water and household soap, would know better how to reward a victory over myself than to help me in my daily efforts.

And what of my approaching departure? And freedom? Ah, no! The only moment when freedom is truly dazzling is at the dawn of love, of first love, when you can say, as you offer it to the person you love: 'Take! I wish I could give you more.'

As for the new cities and new countrysides, so briefly glimpsed, so quickly passed that they grow blurred in the memory, are there such things as new countries for one who spins round and round in circles like a bird held on a string? Will not my pathetic flight, begun anew each morning, inevitably end up each evening at the fatal 'first-class establishment' which Salomon and Brague praise so highly to me?

I have seen so many 'first-class establishments' already! On the side of the public there is an auditorium cruelly flooded with light, where the heavy smoke hardly tones down the gilt of the mouldings. On the artistes' side there are sordid, airless cells, and a staircase leading to filthy lavatories.

Must I really, for forty days, endure this struggle against fatigue, the bantering ill-will of the stage-heads, the raging pride of provincial conductors, the inadequate fare of hotels and stations? Must I discover and perpetually renew in myself that rich fund of energy which is essential to the life of wanderers and solitaries? Must I, in short, struggle—ah, how could I forget it?—against solitude itself? And to achieve what? What? What?

When I was small they said to me: 'Effort brings its own reward,' and so, whenever I had tried specially hard, I used to expect a mysterious, overwhelming recompense, a sort of grace to which I should have surrendered myself. I am still expecting it.

The muffled trill of a bell, followed by the barking of my dog, delivers me at last from this bitter reverie. And suddenly I am on my feet, surprised to find I have jumped lightly up and begun quite simply to live again.

'Madame,' says Blandine in a low voice, 'may M. Dufferein-Chautel come in?'

'No . . . just a minute.'

To powder my cheeks, redden my lips, and comb out the tangled locks which hide my forehead is a rapid mechanical task which does not even need the help of a mirror. One does it as one brushes one's nails, more for manners than vanity.

'Are you there, Dufferein-Chautel? You can come in. Wait a moment, I'll turn on the light.'

I feel no embarrassment at seeing him again. The fact that our mouths met yesterday, abortively, does not make me feel the least awkward at this moment. A bungled kiss is much less important than an understanding exchange of looks. And I almost feel surprised that he for his part should look unhappy and frustrated. I called him Dufferein-Chautel as usual, as though he had no Christian name. I always call him 'You' or 'Dufferein-Chautel.' Is it for me to put him at his ease? I suppose it is.

'So there you are! Are you well?'

'Thank you, I'm well.'

'You don't look it.'

'That's because I'm unhappy,' he does not fail to reply.

Really, what a Big-Noodle! I smile at his unhappiness, the trifling unhappiness of a man who has embraced clumsily the woman he loves. I smile at him from rather far away, from the other side of the chaste black stream where I was bathing a while back. I hand him a little vase filled with his favourite cigarettes, made of a sweet, golden tobacco which smells like spice-bread.

'You're not smoking today?'

'Yes, of course. But I'm unhappy all the same.'

Sitting on the divan, with his back against the low cushions, he exhales at regular intervals long jets of smoke from his nostrils. I smoke too, for something to do and to keep him company. He looks better bare-headed. A top-hat makes him uglier and a soft felt handsomer to the point of flashiness. He smokes with his eyes on the ceiling, as though the seriousness of the words he is preparing prevented him from paying any attention to me. His long, shining eyelashes—the one sensuous, feminine ornament of that face whose fault is excess of virility—blink frequently, betraying agitation and hesitancy. I can hear him breathing. I can also hear the tick-tock of my little travelling-clock, and the screen in the fireplace which the wind suddenly rattles.

'Is it raining outside?'

'No,' he says with a start. 'Why do you ask me that?'

'So's to know. I haven't been out since lunch, I don't know what the weather's like.'

'Just ordinary . . . Renée!'

All of a sudden he sits up and throws away his cigarette. He takes my hands and looks very closely at me, so closely that his face appears to me almost too big, with the details strongly emphasized, the texture of the skin, and the moist and quivering corner of his large eyes. What love there is, yes, love, in those eyes! How speaking they are, and gentle, and wholly enamoured! And those big hands which clasp mine with such steady, communicative strength, how much in earnest I feel them!

It is the first time that I leave my hands in his. At first I feel I have to overcome my repugnance, then their warmth reassures and persuades me, and in a moment I shall yield to the surprising, brotherly pleasure, for so long unfamiliar, of confiding without words in a friend, of leaning for a moment against him, of finding comfort in the nearness of a warm, motionless being, affectionate and silent. Oh, to throw my arms round the neck of a creature, dog or man, a creature who loves me!

'Renée! What is it, Renée, you're not crying?'

'Am I crying?'

He's quite right, I am! The light dances in my brimming tears in a thousand broken, criss-cross rays. I wipe them quickly with a corner of my handkerchief, but I don't dream of denying them. And I smile at the idea that I was about to cry. How long is it since last I cried? It must be years and years.

My friend is overcome. He draws me towards him and forces me—not that I protest much—to sit beside him on the divan. His eyes, too, are moist. After all he is only a man, capable of feigning an emotion, no doubt, but not of hiding it.

'My darling child, what is the matter?'

Will he forget the stifled cry, the shudder which answers him? I hope so. 'My darling child!' His first word of tenderness is 'My darling child!' The same word and almost the same accent as *the other* . . .

A childish fear wrenches me from his arms, as if *the other* had just appeared at the door with his Kaiser William moustache, his false, veiled gaze, his terrible shoulders, and his short, peasant's thighs.

'Renée, my darling, if only you would talk to me a little!'

My friend is quite pale and does not try to take me in his arms again. May he at least never know the pain he has just, so innocently, given me! I no longer want to cry. My delicious, cowardly tears slowly return to their source, leaving a burning sensation in my eyes and throat. While I wait for my voice to steady itself, I reassure my friend with a nod.

'I've made you angry, Renée?'

'No, my friend.'

I sit down beside him again, of my own accord, but timidly, for fear my gesture and my words should provoke another tender exclamation as familiar and hateful as the last.

His instinct warns him not to rejoice at my sudden docility. I feel no desire to embrace me in the arm which supports me, and the dangerous, grateful communicative warmth is no longer there. No doubt he loves me enough to guess that, if I lay an obedient head on his strong shoulder, it is a question of a trial more than a gift.

Can this be my forehead on a man's shoulder? Am I dreaming? I am neither dreaming nor wandering. Both my head and my senses are calm, ominously calm. Yet there is something better and more than indifference in the ease which keeps me there, and the fact that I can let my hand play innocently and unthinkingly with the plaited gold chain on his waistcoat shows that I feel myself sheltered and protected, like the lost cat one rescues, who only knows how to play and sleep when it has a house.

Poor admirer . . . I wonder what he is thinking of as he sits there motionless, respecting my silence? I lean my head back to look at him, but immediately lower my lids, dazzled and abashed by the expression on this man's face. Ah, how I envy him for loving so deeply, for the passion that confers such beauty on him!

His eyes meet mine and he smiles bravely.

'Renée . . . do you think a time will ever come when you will love me?'

'Love you? How I wish I could, my friend! *You*, at least, don't look cruel. Don't you feel that I am beginning to get fond of you?'

'To get fond of me . . . that's just what I'm afraid of, Renée; that hardly ever leads to love.'

He is so profoundly right that I do not protest.

'But . . . be patient . . . you never know. It may be that, when I come back from my tour . . . And then, after all, a great, great friendship . . .'

He shakes his head. Obviously he has no use for my friendship. For my part I should be very glad to have a friend who was less old, less *worn out*, than Hamond, a real friend . . .

'When you come back . . . In the first place, if you really hoped to love me one day, Renée, you wouldn't think of going away from me. In two months' time, just as now, it will be the same Renée who will stretch out her cold little hands, with eyes that shut me out, and that mouth which, even when it offers its lips, does not surrender itself.'

'It's not my fault. Yet here it is, this mouth. See . . .'

With my head on his shoulder once more, I close my eyes, more resigned than curious, only to open them again at the end of a moment, surprised that he does not swoop down with the greedy haste of yesterday. All he has done is to turn a little towards me and encircle me comfortably with his right arm. Then he gathers my two hands into his free hand and bends forward, and I see slowly approaching the serious unfamiliar face of this man whom I know so little.

Now there is hardly any space or air between our two faces, and I try and jerk myself free, breathing fast as if I were drowning. But he holds my hands and tightens his arm round my waist. In vain I bend my neck back, just at the moment when Maxime's mouth reaches mine.

I have not closed my eyes. I frown in an attempt to threaten those eyes above me, which try to subjugate and extinguish mine. For the lips which kiss me are just the same as yesterday, gentle, cool, and impersonal, and their ineffectiveness irritates me. But all of a sudden they change, and now I no longer recognize the kiss, which quickens, insists, falters, then begins again with a rhythmical movement, and finally stops as if waiting for a response which does not come.

I move my head imperceptibly, because of his moustache which brushes against my nostrils with a scent of vanilla and honeyed tobacco. Oh! . . . suddenly my mouth, in spite of itself, lets itself be opened, opens of itself as irresistibly as a ripe plum splits in the sun. And once again there is born that exacting pain that spreads from my lips, all down my flanks as far as my knees, that swelling as of a wound that wants to open once more and overflow—the voluptuous pleasure that I had forgotten.

I let the man who has awakened me drink the fruit he is pressing. My hands, stiff a moment ago, lie warm and soft in his, and my body, as I lie back, strives to mould itself to his. Drawn close by the arm which holds me, I burrow deeper into his shoulder and press myself against him, taking care not to separate our lips and to prolong our kiss comfortably.

He understands and assents, with a happy little grunt. Sure at last that I shall not flee, it is he who breaks away from me, to draw breath and contemplate me as he bites his moist lips. I let my lids fall, since I no longer need to see him. Is he going to undress me and take possession of me completely? It doesn't matter. I am lapped in a lazy, irresponsible joy. The only urgent thing is that that kiss should begin again. We have all our time. Full of pride, my friend gathers me up is his arms as though I were a bunch of flowers, and half lays me on the divan where he rejoins me. His mouth tastes of mine now, and has the faint scent of my powder. Experienced as it is, I can feel that it is trying to invent something new, to vary the caress still further. But already I am bold enough to indicate my preference for a long, drowsy kiss that is almost motionless—the slow crushing, one against the other, of two flowers in which nothing vibrates but the palpitation of two coupled pistils.

And now comes a great truce when we rest and get our breath back. This time it was I who left him, and got up because I felt the need to open my arms, to draw myself up and stretch. Anxious to arrange my hair and see what my new face looked like, I took up the hand-mirror, and it makes me laugh to see we both have the same sleepy features, the same trembling, shiny, slightly swollen lips. Maxime has remained on the divan and his mute appeal receives the most flattering of responses: my look of a submissive bitch, rather shame-faced, rather cowed, very much petted, and ready to accept the leash, the collar, the place at her master's feet, and everything.

THE WAITING SUPPER

SUPPER

THOMAS HARDY

*In their youth, the lovers in Thomas Hardy's story
have their love threatened by their own pride, and the
conventions of the day. But when, later in life, society
comes between them again, they forge a different
kind of connection, unexpected but
just as powerful.*

Whoever had perceived the yeoman's tall figure standing on Squire Everard's lawn in the dusk of that October evening fifty years ago, might have said at first sight that he was loitering there from idle curiosity. For a large five-light window of the manor-house in front of him was unshuttered and uncurtained, so that the illuminated room within could be scanned almost to its four corners. Obviously nobody was ever expected to be in this part of the grounds after nightfall.

The apartment thus commanded by an eye from without was occupied by two persons only; they were sitting over dessert, the tablecloth having been removed in the old-fashioned way. The fruits were local, consisting of apples, pears, nuts, and such other products of the summer as might be presumed to grow on the estate. There was strong ale and rum on the table, and but little wine. Moreover, the appointments of the dining-room were simple and homely even for the date, betokening a countrified household of the smaller gentry, without much wealth or ambition—formerly a numerous class, but now in great part ousted by the territorial landlords.

One of the two sitters was a young lady in white muslin, who listened somewhat impatiently to the remarks of her companion, an elderly, rubicund personage, whom the merest stranger could have pronounced to be her father. The watcher evinced no signs of moving, and it became evident that affairs were not so simple as they first had seemed. The tall farmer was in fact no accidental spectator, and he stood by premeditation close to the trunk of a tree, so that had any traveller passed along the road without the park gate, or even along the drive to the door, that person would scarce have noticed the other, notwithstanding that the gate was quite near at hand, and the park little larger than a paddock. There was still light enough in the western heaven to faintly brighten one side of the man's face, and to show against the dark mass of foliage behind the admirable cut of his profile; also to reveal that the front of the manor-house, small though it seemed, was solidly built of stone in that never-to-be-surpassed style for the English country residence—the mullioned and transomed Elizabethan.

The lawn, although neglected, was still as level as a bowling-green—which indeed it might once have served for; and the blades of grass before the window were raked by the candle-shine, which stretched over them so far as to touch faintly the yeoman's face on that side.

Within the dining-room there were also, with one of the twain, the same signs of a hidden purpose that marked the farmer. The young lady's mind was straying as clearly into the shadows as that of the loiterer was fixed upon the room—nay, it could be said that she was even cognisant of the presence of him outside. Impatience caused her little foot to beat silently on the carpet, and she more than once rose to leave the table. This proceeding was checked by her father, who would put his hand upon her shoulder, and unceremoniously press her down into her chair, till he should have concluded his observations. Her replies were brief enough, and there was factitiousness in her smiles of assent to his views. A small iron casement between two of the mullions was open, so that some occasional words of the dialogue were audible without.

'As for drains—how can I put in drains? The pipes don't cost much, that's true; but the labour in sinking the trenches is ruination. And then the gates—they should be hung to stone posts, otherwise there's no keeping them up through harvest.' The Squire's voice was strongly toned with the local accent, so that he said 'draïns' and 'gents' like the rustics on his estate.

The landscape without grew darker, and the young man's figure seemed to be absorbed into the trunk of the tree. The small stars filled in between the larger, the nebulae between the small stars, the trees quite lost their voice; and if there was still a sound, it was the purl of a stream which stretched along under the trees that bounded the lawn on its northern side.

At last the young girl did get to her feet, and so secured her retreat. 'I have something to do, papa,' she said. 'I shall not be in the drawing-room just yet.'

'Very well,' replied he. 'Then I won't hurry.' And closing

the door behind her, he drew his decanters together, and settled down in his chair.

Three minutes after that, a female shape emerged from a little garden-door which admitted from the lawn to the entrance front, and came across the grass. She kept well clear of the dining-room window, but enough of its light fell on her to show, escaping from the long dark-hooded cloak that she wore, stray verges of the same light dress which had figured but recently at the dinner-table. The hood was contracted tight about her face with a drawing-string, making her countenance small and baby-like, and lovelier even than before.

Without hesitation she brushed across the grass to the tree under which the young man stood concealed. The moment she had reached him he enclosed her form with his arm. The meeting and embrace, though by no means formal, were yet not passionate; the whole proceeding was that of persons who had repeated the act so often as to be unconscious of its performance. She turned within his arm, and faced in the same direction with himself, which was towards the window; and thus they stood without speaking, the back of her head leaning against his shoulder. For a while each seemed to be thinking his and her diverse thoughts.

'You have kept me waiting a long time, dear Christine,' he said at last. 'I wanted to speak to you particularly, or I should not have stayed. How came you to be dining at this time o' night?'

'My father has been out all day, and dinner was put back till five o'clock. I know I have kept you; but Nicholas, how can I help it sometimes, if I am not to run any risk? My poor father insists upon my listening to all he has to say; since my brother left he has had nobody else to listen to him; and tonight he was particularly tedious on his usual topics—draining, and tenant-farmers, and the village people. I must take daddy to London; he gets so narrow always staying here.'

'And what did you say to it all?'

'Oh, I took the part of the tenant-farmers, of course, as the beloved of one should in duty do.' There followed a little break or gasp, implying a strangled sigh.

'You are sorry you have encouraged that beloving one?'

'O no, Nicholas . . . What is it you want to see me for particularly?'

'I know you *are* sorry, as time goes on, and everything is at a dead lock, with no prospect of change, and your rural swain loses his freshness! Only think, this secret understanding between us has lasted near three year, ever since you was a little over sixteen.'

'Yes; it has been a long time.'

'And I an untamed uncultivated man, who has never seen London, and who knows nothing about society at all.'

'Not uncultivated, dear Nicholas. Untravelled, socially unpractised, if you will,' she said smiling. 'Well, I did sigh; but not because I regret being your plighted one. What I do sometimes regret is that the scheme, which my meetings with you are but a part of, has not been carried out in its entirety. You said, Nicholas, that if I consented to swear to keep faith with you, you would go away and travel, and see nations, and peoples, and cities, and take a professor with you, and study books and art, simultaneously with your study of men and manners; and then come back at the end of two years, when I should find that my father would by no means be indisposed to accept you as a son-in-law. You said your reason for wishing to get my promise before starting was that your mind would then be more at rest when you were far away, and so could give itself more completely to knowledge, than if you went as my unaccepted lover only, fuming with anxiety as to my favour when you came back. I saw how reasonable that was; and solemnly plighted myself to you in consequence. But instead of going to see the world, you stay on and on here to see me.'

'And you don't want me to see you?'

'Yes—no—it is not that. It is that I have latterly felt frightened at what I am doing when not in your actual presence. It seems so wicked not to tell my father that I have a lover close at hand, within touch and view of both of us; whereas, if you were absent my conduct would not seem quite so treacherous. The realities would not stare at one so. You would be a pleasant dream to me, which I should be free to indulge in without reproach of my conscience; I should live in hopeful expectation of your returning fully qualified to boldly claim me of my father. There, I have been terribly frank, I know.'

He in his turn had lapsed into gloomy breathings now. 'I did plan it as you state,' he answered. 'I did mean to go away the moment I had your promise. But, dear Christine, I did not foresee two or three things. I did not know what a lot of pain it would cost to tear myself from you. And I did not know that my miserly uncle—heaven forgive me calling him so!—would so positively refuse to advance me money for my purpose—the scheme of travelling with an accomplished tutor costing a formidable sum o' money. You have no idea what it would cost!'

'But I have said that I'll find the money.'

'Ah, there,' he returned 'you have hit a sore place. To speak truly, dear, I would rather stay unpolished a hundred years than take your money.'

'But why? Men continually use the money of the women they marry.'

'Yes; but not till afterwards. No man would like to touch your money at present, and I should feel very mean if I were to do so in present circumstances. That brings me to what I was going to propose. But no—upon the whole I will not propose it now.'

'Ah! I would guarantee expenses, and you won't let me! The money is my personal possession: it comes to me from my late grandfather, and not from my father at all.'

He laughed forcedly and pressed her hand. 'There are more reasons why I cannot tear myself away,' he added. 'What would become of my uncle's farming? Six hundred acres in this parish, and five hundred in the next—a constant traipsing from one farm to the other; he can't be in two places at once. Still, that might be got over if it were not for the other matters. Besides, dear, I still should be a little uneasy, even though I have your promise, lest somebody should snap you up away from me.'

'Ah, you should have thought of that before. Otherwise I have committed myself for nothing.'

'I should have thought of it,' he answered, gravely. 'But I did not. There lies my fault, I admit it freely. Ah, if you would only commit yourself a little more, I might at least get over that difficulty! But I won't ask you. You have no idea how much you are to me still; you could not argue so coolly if you had. What property belongs to you I hate the very sound of; it is you I care for. I wish you hadn't a farthing in the world but what I could earn for you!'

'I don't altogether wish that,' she murmured.

'I wish it, because it would have made what I was going to propose much easier to do than it is now. Indeed I will not propose it, although I came on purpose, after what you have said in your frankness.'

'Nonsense, Nic. Come, tell me. How can you be so touchy!'

'Look at this then, Christine dear.' He drew from his breast-pocket a sheet of paper and unfolded it, when it was observable that a seal dangled from the bottom.

'What is it?' She held the paper sideways, so that what there was of window-light fell on its surface. 'I can only read the old-English letters—why—our names! Surely it is not a marriage-licence?'

'It is.'

She trembled. 'Oh, Nic; how could you do this—and without telling me!'

'Why should I have thought I must tell you? You had not spoken "frankly" then as you have now. We have been all to each other more than these two years, and I thought I would propose that we marry privately, and that I then leave you on the instant. I would have taken my travelling-bag to church, and you would have gone home alone. I should not have started on my adventures in the brilliant manner of our original plan, but should have roughed it a little at first; my great gain would have been that the absolute possession of you would have enabled me to work with spirit and purpose, such as nothing else could do. But I dare not ask you now—so frank as you have been.'

She did not answer. The document he had produced gave such unexpected substantiality to the venture with which she had so long toyed as a vague dream merely, that she was, in truth, frightened a little. 'I—don't know about it!' she said.

'Perhaps not. Ah, my little lady, you are wearying of me!'

'No, Nic,' responded she, creeping closer. 'I am not. Upon my word, and truth, and honour, I am not, Nic.'

'A mere tiller of the soil, as I should be called,' he continued, without heeding her. 'And you—well, a daughter of one of the—I won't say oldest families, because that's absurd, all families are the same age—one of the longest chronicled families about here, whose name is actually the name of the place.'

'That's not much, I am sorry to say! My poor brother— but I won't speak of that . . . Well,' she murmured mischievously, after a pause, 'you certainly would not need to be uneasy if I were to do this that you want me to do. You would have me safe enough in your trap then; I couldn't get away!'

'That's just it!' he said vehemently. 'It *is* a trap—you feel it so, and that though you wouldn't be able to get away from me you might particularly wish to! Ah, if I had asked you two years ago you would have agreed instantly. But I thought I was bound to wait for the proposal to come from you as the superior!'

'Now you are angry, and take seriously what I meant purely in fun. You don't know me even yet! To show you that you have not been mistaken in me, I *do* propose to carry out this licence. I'll marry you, dear Nicholas, tomorrow morning.'

'Ah, Christine! I am afraid I have stung you on to this, so that I cannot—'

'No, no, no!' she hastily rejoined; and there was something in her tone which suggested that she had been put upon her mettle and would not flinch. 'Take me whilst I am in the humour. What church is the licence for?'

'That I've not looked to see—why our parish church here, of course. Ah, then we cannot use it! We dare not be married here.'

'We do dare,' said she. 'And we will too, if you'll be there.'

'*If* I'll be there!'

They speedily came to an agreement that he should be in the church-porch at ten minutes to eight on the following morning, awaiting her; and that, immediately after the conclusion of the service which would make them one, Nicholas should set out on his long-deferred educational tour, towards the cost of which she was resolving to bring a substantial subscription with her to church. Then, slipping from him, she went indoors by the way she had come, and Nicholas bent his steps homewards.

II

Instead of leaving the lawn by the gate, he flung himself over the fence, and pursued a direction towards the river under the trees. And it was now, in his lonely progress, that he showed for the first time outwardly that he was not altogether unworthy of her. He wore long water-boots reaching above his knees, and, instead of making a circuit to find a bridge by which he might cross the Swenn—as the river aforesaid was called—he made straight for the point whence proceeded the low roar that was at this hour the only evidence of the stream's existence. He speedily stood on the verge of the waterfall which caused the noise, and stepping into the water at the top of the same, waded through with the sure tread of one who knew every inch of his footing, even though the canopy of trees rendered the darkness almost absolute, and a false step would have precipitated him into the pool beneath. Soon reaching the boundary of the grounds, he continued in the same direct line to traverse the alluvial valley, full of brooks and tributaries to the main stream—in former times quite impassable, and impassable in winter now. Sometimes he would cross a deep gulley on a plank not wider than the hand; at another time he ploughed his way through beds of spear-grass, where at a few feet to the right or left he might have been sucked down into a morass. At last he reached firm land on the other side of this watery tract, and came to his house on the rise behind—an ordinary farmstead, from the back of which rose indistinct breathings, belchings, and snortings, the rattle of halters, and other familiar features of an agriculturist's home.

While Nicholas Long was packing his bag in an upper room of this dwelling, Miss Christine Everard sat at a desk in her own chamber at Swenn-Everard manor-house, looking with pale fixed countenance at the candles.

'I ought—I must now!' she whispered to herself. 'I should not have begun it if I had not meant to carry it through! It runs in the blood of us, I suppose.' She alluded to a fact unknown to her lover, the clandestine marriage of an aunt under circumstances somewhat similar to the present. In a few minutes she had penned the following note:—

'October 13, 1838.

'DEAR MR. EASTMAN,—Can you make it convenient to yourself to meet me at the Church tomorrow morning at eight? I name the early hour because it would suit me better than later on in the day. You will find me in the chancel, if you can come. An answer yes or no by the bearer of this will be sufficient.

'CHRISTINE EVERARD.'

She sent the note to the rector immediately, waiting at a small side-door of the house till she heard the servant's footsteps returning along the lane, when she went round and met him in the passage. The rector had taken the trouble to write a line, and answered that he would meet her with pleasure.

A dripping fog which ushered in the next morning was highly favourable to the scheme of the pair. At that time of the century Swenn-Everard House had not been altered into a farm-homestead; the public lane passed close under its walls; and there was a door opening directly from one of the old parlours—the south parlour, as it was called—into the lane which led to the village. Christine came out this way, and after following the lane for a short distance entered upon a path within a belt of plantation, by which the church could be reached privately. She even avoided the churchyard gate, walking along to a place where the turf without the low wall rose into a mound, enabling her to mount upon the coping and spring down inside. She crossed the wet graves, and so glided round to the door. He was there, with his bag in his hand. He kissed her with a sort of surprise, as if he had expected that at the last moment her heart would fail her.

Though it had not failed her, there was, nevertheless, no great ardour in Christine's bearing—merely the momentum of an antecedent impulse. They went up the aisle together, the bottle-green glass of the old lead quarries admitting but little light at that hour, and under such an atmosphere. They stood by the altar-rail in silence, Christine's skirt visibly quivering at each beat of her heart.

Presently a quick step ground upon the gravel, and Mr Eastman came round by the front. He was a quiet bachelor, courteous towards Christine, and not at first recognizing in Nicholas a neighbouring yeoman (for he lived in a remote part of the parish), advanced to her without revealing any surprise at her unusual request. But in truth he was surprised, the keen interest taken by many country young women at the present day in church decoration and festivals being then unknown.

'Good morning,' he said; and repeated the same words to Nicholas more mechanically.

'Good morning,' she replied gravely. 'Mr Eastman, I have a serious reason for asking you to meet me—us, I may say. We wish you to marry us.'

The rector's gaze hardened to fixity, rather between than upon either of them, and he neither moved nor replied for some time.

'Ah!' he said at last.

'And we are quite ready.'

'I had no idea—'

'It has been kept rather private,' she said calmly.

'Where are your witnesses?'

'They are outside in the meadow, sir. I can call them in a moment,' said Nicholas.

'Oh—I see it is—Mr Nicholas Long,' said Mr Eastman, and turning again to Christine, 'Does your father know of this?'

'Is it necessary that I should answer that question, Mr. Eastman?'

'I am afraid it is—highly necessary.'

Christine began to look concerned.

'Where is the licence?' the rector asked; 'since there have been no banns.'

Nicholas produced it, Mr Eastman read it, an operation

which occupied him several minutes—or at least he made it appear so; till Christine said impatiently, 'We are quite ready, Mr Eastman. Will you proceed? Mr Long has to take a journey of a great many miles today.'

'And you?'

'No. I remain.'

Mr Eastman assumed firmness. 'There is something wrong in this,' he said. 'I cannot marry you without your father's presence.'

'But have you a right to refuse us?' interposed Nicholas. 'I believe we are in a position to demand your fulfilment of our request.'

'No you are not! Is Miss Everard of age? I think not. I think she is far from being so. Eh, Miss Everard?'

'Am I bound to tell that?'

'Certainly. At any rate you are bound to write it. Meanwhile I refuse to solemnize the service. And let me entreat you two young people to do nothing so rash as this, even if by going to some strange church, you may do so without discovery. The tragedy of marriage—'

'Tragedy?'

'Certainly. It is full of crises and catastrophes, and ends with the death of one of the actors. The tragedy of marriage, as I was saying, is one I shall not be a party to your beginning with such light hearts, and I shall feel bound to put your father on his guard, Miss Everard. Think better of it, I entreat you! Remember the proverb, "Marry in haste and repent at leisure."'

Christine grew passionate, almost stormed at him. Nicholas implored; but nothing would turn that obstinate rector. She sat down and painfully reflected. By-and-bye she confronted Mr Eastman.

'Our marriage is not to be this morning, I see,' she said. 'Now grant me one favour, and in return I'll promise you to do nothing rashly. Do not tell my father a word of what has happened here.'

'I agree—if you undertake not to elope.'

She looked at Nicholas, and he looked at her. 'Do you wish me to elope, Nic?' she asked.

'No,' he said.

So the compact was made and they left the church singly, Nicholas remaining till the last, and closing the door. On his way home, carrying the well-packed bag which was just now to go no further, the two men who were mending water-carriers in the meadows approached the hedge, as if they had been on the alert all the time.

'You said you mid want us for zummat, sir?'

'All right—never mind,' he answered through the hedge. 'I did not require you after all.'

• • •

III

At a neighbouring manor there lived a queer and primitive couple who had lately been blessed with a son and heir. The christening took place during the week under notice, and this had been followed by a feast to the parishioners. Christine's father, one of the same generation and kind, had been asked to drive over and assist in the entertainment, and Christine, as a matter of course, accompanied him.

When they reached Eldhampton Hall, as the house was called, they found the usually quiet nook a lively spectacle. Tables had been spread in the apartment which lent its name to the whole building—the hall proper—covered with a fine open-timbered roof, whose braces, purlins and rafters made a brown thicket of oak overhead. Here tenantry of all ages sat with their wives and families, and the servants were assisted in their ministrations by the sons and daughters of the owner's friends and neighbours. Christine lent a hand among the rest.

She was holding a plate in each hand towards a huge brown platter of baked rice-pudding, from which a footman was scooping a large spoonful, when a voice reached her ear over her shoulder: 'Allow me to hold them for you.'

Christine turned, and recognized in the speaker the nephew of the entertainer, a young man from London, whom she had already met on two or three occasions. She accepted the proffered help, and from that moment, whenever he passed her in their marchings to and fro during the remainder of the serving, he smiled acquaintance. When their work was done, he improved the few words into a conversation. He plainly had been attracted by her fairness.

Bellston was a self-assured young man, not particularly good-looking, with more colour in his skin than even Nicholas had. He had flushed a little in attracting her notice, though the flush had nothing of nervousness in it—the air with which it was accompanied making it curiously suggestive of a flush of anger; and even when he laughed it was difficult to banish that fancy.

The rich autumn sunlight streamed in through the window-panes upon the heads and shoulders of the venerable patriarchs of the hamlet, and upon the middle-aged, and upon the young; upon men and women who had played out, or were to play, tragedies or tragi-comedies in that nook of civilization not less great, humanly, than those which, enacted on more central arenas, fix the attention of the world. One of the party was a cousin of Nicholas Long's, who sat with her husband and children.

To make himself as locally harmonious as possible, Mr Bellston remarked to his companion on the scene—

'It does one's heart good,' he said, 'to see these simple peasants enjoying themselves.'

'Oh, Mr Bellston!' exclaimed Christine; 'don't be too sure about that word "simple"! You little think what they see

and meditate! Their reasonings and emotions are as complicated as ours.'

She spoke with a vehemence which would have been hardly
present in her words but for her own relation to Nicholas. The
sense of that produced in her a nameless depression thence-
forward. The young man, however, still followed her up.

'I am glad to hear you say it,' he returned warmly. 'I was
merely attuning myself to your mood, as I thought. The real
truth is that I know more of the Parthians, and Medes, and
dwellers in Mesopotamia—almost of any people, indeed—
than of the English rustics. Travel and exploration are my
profession, not the study of the British peasantry.'

Travel. There was sufficient coincidence between his
declaration and the course she had urged upon her lover, to
lend Bellston's account of himself a certain interest in
Christine's ears. He might perhaps be able to tell her something that would be useful to Nicholas, if their dream were
carried out. A door opened from the hall into the garden, and
she somehow found herself outside, chatting with Mr
Bellston on this topic, till she thought that, upon the whole,
she liked the young man. The garden being his uncle's, he
took her round it with an air of proprietorship; and they went
on amongst the Michaelmas-daisies and chrysanthemums,
and through a door to the fruit-garden. A green-house was
open, and he went in and cut her a bunch of grapes.

'How daring of you! They are your uncle's.'

'Oh, he don't mind—I do anything here. A rough old buffer, isn't he?'

She was thinking of her Nic, and felt that by comparison with her present acquaintance, the farmer more than held his own as a fine and intelligent fellow; but the harmony with her own existence in little things, which she found here, imparted an alien tinge to Nicholas just now. The latter, idealized by moonlight, or a thousand miles of distance, was altogether a more romantic object for a woman's dream than this smart new-lacquered man; but in the sun of afternoon, and amid a surrounding company, Mr Bellston was a very tolerable companion.

When they re-entered the hall, Bellston entreated her to come with him up a spiral stair in the thickness of the wall, leading to a passage and gallery, whence they could look down upon the scene below. The people had finished their feast, the newly-christened baby had been exhibited, and a few words having been spoken to them they began, amid a racketing of forms, to make for the greensward without, Nicholas's cousin and cousin's wife and cousin's children among the rest. While they were filing out, a voice was heard calling—

'Hullo!—here, Jim; where are you?' said Bellston's uncle. The young man descended, Christine following at leisure.

'Now will ye be a good fellow,' the Squire continued, 'and set them going outside in some dance or other that they know? I'm dead tired, and I want to have a few words with Mr Everard before we join 'em—hey, Everard? They are shy till somebody starts 'em; afterwards they'll keep gwine brisk enough.'

'Ay, that they wool,' said Squire Everard.

They followed to the lawn; and here it proved that James Bellston was as shy, or rather as averse, as any of the tenantry themselves, to acting the part of fugleman. Only the parish people had been at the feast, but outlying neighbours had now strolled in for a dance.

'They want "Speed the Plough",' said Bellston, coming up breathless. 'It must be a country dance, I suppose? Now, Miss Everard, do have pity upon me. I am supposed to lead off; but really I know no more about speeding the plough than a child just born! Would you take one of the villagers?—just to start them, my uncle says. Suppose you take that handsome young farmer over there—I don't know his name, but I dare say you do—and I'll come on with one of the dairyman's daughters as second couple.'

Christine turned in the direction signified, and changed colour—though in the shade nobody noticed it. 'Oh, yes—I know him,' she said coolly. 'He is from our own place—Mr Nicholas Long.'

'That's capital—then you can easily make him stand as first couple with you. Now I must pick up mine.'

'I—I think I'll dance with you, Mr Bellston,' she said with

some trepidation. 'Because, you see,' she explained eagerly, 'I know the figure, and you don't—so that I can help you; while Nicholas Long, I know, is familiar with the figure, and that will make two couples who know it—which is necessary, at least.'

Bellston showed his gratification by one of his angry-pleasant flushes—he had hardly dared to ask for what she proffered freely; and having requested Nicholas to take the dairyman's daughter, led Christine to her place, Long promptly stepping up second with his charge. There were grim silent depths in Nic's character; a small deedy spark in his eye, as it caught Christine's, was all that showed his consciousness of her. Then the fiddlers began—the celebrated Mellstock fiddlers who, given free stripping, could play from sunset to dawn without turning a hair. The couples wheeled and swung, Nicholas taking Christine's hand in the course of business with the figure, when she waited for him to give it a little squeeze; but he did not.

Christine had the greatest difficulty in steering her partner through the maze, on account of his self-will, and when at last they reached the bottom of the long line, she was breathless with her hard labour. Resting here, she watched Nic and his lady; and, though she had decidedly cooled off in these later months, began to admire him anew. Nobody knew these dances like him, after all, or could do anything of this sort so well. His performance with the dairyman's daughter so won upon her, that when 'Speed the Plough' was over she contrived to speak to him.

'Nic, you are to dance with me next time.'

He said he would, and presently asked her in a formal public manner, lifting his hat gallantly. She showed a little backwardness, which he quite understood, and allowed him to lead her to the top, a row of enormous length appearing below them as if by magic as soon as they had taken their places. Truly the Squire was right when he said that they only wanted starting.

'What is it to be?' whispered Nicholas.

She turned to the band. '"The Honeymoon",' she said.

And then they trod the delightful last-century measure of that name, which if it had been ever danced better, was never danced with more zest. The perfect responsiveness which their tender acquaintance threw into the motions of Nicholas and his partner lent to their gyrations the fine adjustment of two interacting parts of a single machine. The excitement of the movement carried Christine back to the time—the unreflecting passionate time, about two years before—when she and Nic had been incipient lovers only; and it made her forget the carking anxieties, the vision of social breakers ahead, that had begun to take the gilding off her position now. Nicholas, on his part, had never ceased to be a lover; no personal worries had as yet made him conscious of any staleness, flatness, or unprofitableness in his admiration of Christine.

'Not quite so wildly, Nic,' she whispered. 'I don't object personally; but they'll notice us. How came you here?'

'I heard that you had driven over; and I set out—on purpose for this.'

'What—you have walked?'

'Yes. If I had waited for one of uncle's horses I should have been too late.'

'Eleven miles here and eleven back—two-and-twenty miles on foot—merely to dance!'

'With you. What made you think of this old "Honeymoon" thing?'

'Oh! it came into my head when I saw you, as what would have been a reality with us if you had not been stupid about that licence, and had got it for a distant church.'

'Shall we try again?'

'No—I don't know. I'll think it over.'

The villagers admired their grace and skill, as the dancers themselves perceived; but they did not know what accompanied that admiration in one spot, at least.

'People who wonder they can foot it so featly together should know what some others think,' a waterman was saying to his neighbour. 'Then their wonder would be less.'

His comrade asked for information.

'Well—really I hardly believe it—but 'tis said they be man and wife. Yes, sure—went to church and did the job a'most afore 'twas light one morning. But mind, not a word of this; for 'twould be the loss of a winter's work to me if I had spread such a report and it were not true.'

When the dance had ended she rejoined her own section of the company. Her father and Mr Bellston the elder had now come out from the house, and were smoking in the background. Presently she found that her father was at her elbow.

'Christine, don't dance too often with young Long—as a mere matter of prudence, I mean, as volk might think it odd, he being one of our own parish people. I should not mention this to 'ee if he were an ordinary young fellow; but being superior to the rest it behoves you to be careful.'

'Exactly, papa,' said Christine.

But the revived sense that she was deceiving him threw a damp over her spirits. 'But, after all,' she said to herself, 'he is a young man of Swenn-Everard, handsome, able, and the soul of honour; and I am a young woman of that place, who have been constantly thrown into communication with him. Is it not, by nature's rule, the most proper thing in the world that I should marry him, and is it not an absurd conventional regulation which says that such a union would be wrong?'

It may be concluded that the strength of Christine's large-minded argument was rather an evidence of weakness than of strength in the passion it concerned, which had required neither argument nor reasoning of any kind for its maintenance when full and flush in its early days.

When driving home in the dark with her father, she sank

into pensive silence. She was thinking of Nicholas having to trudge on foot all those eleven miles after his exertions on the sward. Mr Everard, arousing himself from a nap, said suddenly, 'I have something to mention to ye, by George—so I have, Chris! You probably know what it is?'

She wondered if her father had discovered anything of her secret.

'Well, according to *him* you know. But I will tell 'ee. Perhaps you noticed young Jim Bellston walking me off down the lawn with him?—whether or no, we walked together a good while; and he informed me that he wanted to pay his addresses to 'ee. I naturally said that it depended upon yourself; and he replied that you was willing enough; you had given him particular encouragement—showing your preference for him by specially choosing him for your partner—hey? "In that case," says I, "go on and conquer—settle it with her—I have no objection." The poor fellow was very grateful, and in short, there we left the matter. He'll propose tomorrow.'

She saw now to her dismay what James Bellston had read as encouragement. 'He has mistaken me altogether,' she said. 'I had no idea of such a thing.'

'What, you won't have him?'

'Indeed, I cannot!'

'Chrissy,' said Mr Everard with emphasis, 'there's *noo*body whom I should so like you to marry as that young man. He's a thoroughly clever fellow, and fairly well provided for. He's travelled all over the temperate zone; but he says that directly he marries he's going to give up all that, and be a regular stay-at-home. You would be nowhere safer than in his hands.'

'It is true,' she answered. 'He *is* a highly desirable match, and I *should* be well provided for, and probably very safe in his hands.'

'Then don't be skittish, and stand-to.'

She had spoken from her conscience and understanding, and not to please her father. As a reflecting woman she believed that such a marriage would be a wise one. In great things Nicholas was closest to her nature; in little things Bellston seemed immeasurably nearer than Nic; and life was made up of little things.

Altogether the firmament looked black for Nicholas Long, notwithstanding her half-hour's ardour for him when she saw him dancing with the dairyman's daughter. Most great passions, movements, and beliefs—individual and national—burst during their decline into a temporary irradiation, which rivals their original splendour; and then they speedily become extinct. Perhaps the dance had given the last flare-up to Christine's love. It seemed to have improvidently consumed for its immediate purpose all her ardour forwards, so that for the future there was nothing left but frigidity.

Nicholas had certainly been very foolish about that licence!

• • •

IV

This laxity of emotional tone was further increased by an incident, when, two days later, she kept an appointment with Nicholas in the Sallows. The Sallows was an extension of shrubberies and plantations along the banks of the Swenn, accessible from the lawn of Swenn-Everard House only, except by wading through the river at the waterfall or elsewhere. Near the fall was a thicket of box in which a trunk lay prostrate; this had been once or twice their trysting-place, though it was by no means a safe one; and it was here she sat awaiting him now.

The noise of the stream muffled any sound of footsteps, and it was before she was aware of his approach that she looked up and saw him wading across at the top of the waterfall.

Noontide lights and dwarfed shadows always banished the romantic aspect of her love for Nicholas. Moreover, something new had occurred to disturb her; and if ever she had regretted giving way to a tenderness for him—which perhaps she had not done with any distinctness—she regretted it now. Yet in the bottom of their hearts those two were excellently paired, the very twin halves of a perfect whole; and their love was pure. But at this hour surfaces showed garishly, and obscured the depths. Probably her regret appeared in her face.

He walked up to her without speaking, the water running from his boots; and, taking one of her hands in each of his own, looked narrowly into her eyes.

'Have you thought it over?'

'What?'

'Whether we shall try again; you remember saying you would at the dance?'

'Oh, I had forgotten that!'

'You are sorry we tried at all!' he said accusingly.

'I am not so sorry for the fact as for the rumours,' she said.

'Ah! rumours?'

'They say we are already married.'

'Who?'

'I cannot tell exactly. I heard some whispering to that effect. Somebody in the village told one of the servants, I believe. This man said that he was crossing the churchyard early on that unfortunate foggy morning, and heard voices in the chancel, and peeped through the window as well as the dim panes would let him; and there he saw you and me and Mr Eastman, and so on; but thinking his surmises would be dangerous knowledge, he hastened on. And so the story got afloat. Then your aunt, too—'

'Good Lord!—what has she done?'

'The story was told her, and she said proudly. "Oh yes, it is true enough. I have seen the licence. But it is not to be known yet."'

'Seen the licence? How the—'

'Accidentally, I believe, when your coat was hanging somewhere.'

The information, coupled with the infelicitous word 'proudly', caused Nicholas to flush with mortification. He knew that it was in his aunt's nature to make a brag of that sort; but worse than the brag was the fact that this was the first occasion on which Christine had deigned to show her consciousness that such a marriage would be a source of pride to his relatives—the only two he had in the world.

'You are sorry, then, even to be thought my wife, much less to be it.' He dropped her hand, which fell lifelessly.

'It is not sorry exactly, dear Nic. But I feel uncomfortable and vexed, that after screwing up my courage, my fidelity, to the point of going to church, you should have so muddled—managed the matter that it has ended in neither one thing nor the other. How can I meet acquaintances, when I don't know what they are thinking of me?'

'Then, dear Christine, let us mend the muddle. I'll go away for a few days and get another licence, and you can come to me.'

She shrank from this perceptibly. 'I cannot screw myself up to it a second time,' she said. 'I am sure I cannot! Besides, I promised Mr Eastman. And yet how can I continue to see you after such a rumour? We shall be watched now, for certain.'

'Then don't see me.'

'I fear I must not for the present. Altogether—'

'What?'

'I am very depressed.'

These views were not very inspiriting to Nicholas, as he construed them. It may indeed have been possible that he construed them wrongly, and should have insisted upon her making the rumour true. Unfortunately, too, he had come to her in a hurry through brambles and briars, water and weed, and the shaggy wildness which hung about his appearance at this fine and correct time of day lent an impracticability to the look of him.

'You blame me—you repent your courses—you repent that you ever, ever owned anything to me!'

'No, Nicholas, I do not repent that,' she returned gently, though with firmness. 'But I think that you ought not to have got that licence without asking me first; and I also think that you ought to have known how it would be if you lived on here in your present position, and made no effort to better it. I can bear whatever comes, for social ruin is not personal ruin, or even personal disgrace. But as a sensible, new-risen poet says, whom I have been reading this morning—

"The world and its ways have a certain worth:
And to press a point while these oppose
Were simple policy."

'As soon as you had got my promise, Nic, you should have

gone away—yes—and made a name, and come back to claim me. That was my silly girlish dream about my hero.'

'Perhaps I can do as much yet! And would you have indeed liked better to live away from me for family reasons, than to run a risk in seeing me for affection's sake? O what a cold heart it has grown! If I had been a prince, and you a dairymaid, I'd have stood by you in the face of the world!'

She shook her head. 'Ah—you don't know what society is—you don't know.'

'Perhaps not. Who was that strange gentleman of about seven-and-twenty I saw at Mr Bellston's christening feast?'

'Oh—that was his nephew James. Now he is a man who has seen an unusual extent of the world for his age. He is a great traveller, you know.'

'Indeed.'

'In fact an explorer. He is very entertaining.'

'No doubt.'

Nicholas received no shock of jealousy from her announcement. He knew her so well that he could see she was not in the least in love with Bellston. But he asked if Bellston were going to continue his explorations.

'Not if he settles in life. Otherwise he will, I suppose.'

'Perhaps I could be a great explorer, too, if I tried.'

'You could, I am sure.'

They sat apart, and not together; each looking afar off at vague objects, and not in each other's eyes. Thus the sad autumn afternoon waned, while the waterfall hissed sarcastically of the inevitableness of the unpleasant. Very different this from the time when they had first met there.

The nook was most picturesque; but it looked horridly common and stupid now. Their sentiment had set a colour hardly less visible than a material one on surrounding objects, as sentiment must where life is but thought. Nicholas was as devoted as ever to the fair Christine: but unhappily he too had moods and humours; and the division between them was not closed.

She had no sooner got indoors and sat down to her work-table than her father entered the drawing-room. She handed him his newspaper; he took it without a word; went and stood on the hearthrug, and flung the paper on the floor.

'Christine, what's the meaning of this terrible story? I was just on my way to look at the register.'

She looked at him without speech.

'You have married—Nicholas Long?'

'No, father.'

'No? Can you say no in the face of such facts as I have been put in possession of?'

'Yes.'

'But—the note you wrote to the rector—and the going to church?'

She briefly explained that their attempt had failed.

'Ah! Then this is what that dancing meant, was it? By—, it makes me—. How long has this been going on, may I ask?'

'This what?'

'What, indeed? Why, making him your beau. Now listen to me. All's well that ends well; from this day, madam, this moment, he is to be nothing more to you. You are not to see him. Cut him adrift instantly! I only wish his volk were on my farm—out they should go, or I would know the reason why. However, you are to write him a letter to this effect at once.'

'How can I cut him adrift?'

'Why not? You must, my good maid!'

'Well, though I have not actually married him, I have solemnly sworn to be his wife when he comes home from abroad to claim me. It would be gross perjury not to fulfil my promise. Besides, no woman can go to church with a man to deliberately solemnize matrimony, and refuse him afterwards, if he does nothing wrong meanwhile.'

The uttered sound of her strong conviction seemed to kindle in Christine a livelier perception of all its bearings than she had known while it had lain unformulated in her mind. For when she had done speaking she fell down on her knees before her father, covered her face, and said, 'Please, please forgive me, papa! How *could* I do it without letting you know! I don't know, I don't know!'

When she looked up she found that, in the turmoil of his mind, her father was moving about the room. 'You are within an ace of ruining yourself, ruining me, ruining us all!' he said. 'You are nearly as bad as your brother, begad!'

'Perhaps I am—yes—perhaps I am!'

'That I should father such a harum-scarum brood!'

'It is very bad; but Nicholas—'

'He's a scoundrel!'

'He is *not* a scoundrel!' cried she, turning quickly. 'He's as good and worthy as you or I, or anybody bearing our name or any nobleman in the kingdom, if you come to that! Only—only'—she could not continue the argument on those lines. 'Now, father, listen!' she sobbed; 'if you taunt me I'll go off and join him at his farm this very day, and marry him tomorrow, that's what I'll do!'

'I don't taant ye!'

'I wish to avoid unseemliness as much as you.'

She went away. When she came back a quarter of an hour later, thinking to find the room empty, he was standing there as before, never having apparently moved. His manner had quite changed. He seemed to take a resigned and entirely different view of circumstances.

'Christine, I have suffered more in this last haaf hour than I hope you may suffer all your life. But since this was to happen, I'll bear it, and not complain. All volk have crosses, and this is one of mine. Well, this is what I've got to say—I almost feel that you must carry out this attempt at marrying Nicholas Long. Faith, you must! The rumour will become a scandal if you don't—that's my view. I have tried to look at the brightest side of the case. Nicholas Long is a young man superior to most of his class, and fairly presentable. And he's not poor—at least his uncle is not. I believe the old muddler could buy me up any day. However, a farmer's wife you must be, as far as I can see. As you've made your bed, so ye must lie. Parents propose, and ungrateful children dispose. You shall marry him, and immediately.'

Christine hardly knew what to make of this. 'He is quite willing to wait, and so am I. We can wait for two or three years, and then he will be as worthy as—'

'You must marry him. And the sooner the better, if 'tis to be done at all . . . And yet I did wish you could have been Jim Bellston's wife. I did wish it! But no.'

'I did wish it, and do still, in one sense,' she returned gently. His moderation had won her out of her defiant mood, and she was willing to reason with him.

'You do?' he said, surprised.

'I see that in a worldly sense my conduct may be considered a mistake.'

'H'm—I am glad to hear that—after my death you may see it more clearly still; and you won't have long to wait, to my reckoning.'

She fell into bitter repentance, and kissed him in her anguish. 'Don't say that!' she cried. 'Tell me what to do?'

'If you'll leave me for an hour or two I'll think. Drive to

the market and back—the carriage is at the door—and I'll try to collect my senses. Dinner can be put back till you return.'

In a few minutes she was dressed, and the carriage bore her up the hill which divided the village and manor from the market-town.

V

A quarter of an hour brought her into the High Street, and for want of a more important errand she called at the harness-maker's for a dog-collar that she required.

It happened to be market-day, and Nicholas, having postponed the engagements which called him thither to keep the appointment with her in the Sallows, rushed off at the end of the afternoon to attend to them as well as he could. Arriving thus in a great hurry on account of the lateness of the hour, he still retained the wild, amphibious appearance which had marked him when he came up from the meadows to her side—an exceptional condition of things which had scarcely ever before occurred. When she crossed the pavement from the shop door, the shopman bowing and escorting her to the carriage, Nicholas chanced to be standing at the road-waggon office, talking to the master of the waggons. There were a good many people about, and those near paused and looked at her transit, in the full stroke of the level October sun, which went under the brims of their hats, and pierced through their button-holes. From the group she heard murmured the words: 'Mrs Nicholas Long.'

The unexpected remark, not without distinct satire in its tone, took her so greatly by surprise that she was confounded. Nicholas was by this time nearer, though coming against the sun he had not yet perceived her. Influenced by her father's lecture, she felt angry with him for being there and causing this awkwardness. Her notice of him was therefore slight, supercilious perhaps, slurred over; and her vexation at his presence showed distinctly in her face as she sat down in her seat. Instead of catching his waiting eye, she positively turned her head away.

A moment after she was sorry she had treated him so; but he was gone.

Reaching home she found on her dressing-table a note from her father. The statement was brief:

'I have considered and am of the same opinion. You must marry him. He can leave home at once and travel as proposed. I have written to him to this effect. I don't want any victuals, so don't wait dinner for me.'

Nicholas was the wrong sort of man to be blind to his Christine's mortification, though he did not know its entire cause. He had lately foreseen something of this sort as possible.

'It serves me right,' he thought, as he trotted homeward. 'It was absurd—wicked of me to lead her on so. The sacrifice would have been too great—too cruel!' And yet, though he thus took her part, he flushed with indignation every time he said to himself, 'She is ashamed of me!'

On the ridge which overlooked Swenn-Everard he met a neighbour of his—a stock-dealer—in his gig, and they drew rein and exchanged a few words. A part of the dealer's conversation had much meaning for Nicholas.

'I've had occasion to call on Squire Everard,' the former said; 'but he couldn't see me on account of being quite knocked up at some bad news he has heard.'

Nicholas rode on past Swenn-Everard to Homeston Farm, pondering. He had new and startling matter for thought as soon as he got there. The Squire's note had arrived. At first he could not credit its import; then he saw further, took in the tone of the letter, saw the writer's contempt behind the words, and understood that the letter was written as by a man hemmed into a corner. Christine was defiantly—insultingly—hurled at his head. He was accepted because he was so despised.

And yet with what respect he had treated her and hers! Now he was reminded of what an agricultural friend had said years ago, when the eyes of Nicholas were once fixed on Christine as on an angel as she passed: 'Better a little fire to warm ye than a great one to burn ye. No good can come of throwing your heart there.' He went into the mead, sat down, and asked himself four questions:—

1. How could she live near her acquaintance as his wife, even in his absence, without suffering martyrdom from the stings of their contempt?

2. Would not this entail total estrangement between Christine and her family also, and her own consequent misery?

3. Must not such isolation extinguish her affection for him?

4. Supposing that her father rigged them out as colonists and sent them off to America, was not the effect of such exile upon one of her gentle nurture likely to be as the last?

In short, whatever they should embark in together would be cruelty to her, and his death would be a relief. It would, indeed, in one aspect be a relief to her now, if she were so ashamed of him as she had appeared to be that day. Were he dead, this little episode with him would fade away like a dream.

Mr Everard was a good-hearted man at bottom, but to take his enraged offer seriously was impossible. The least thing that he could do would be to go away and never trouble her more. To travel and learn and come back in two years, as mapped out in their first sanguine scheme, required a staunch heart on her side, if the necessary expenditure of time and money were to be afterwards justified; and it were folly to calculate on that when he had seen today that her heart was failing her already. To travel and disappear and not be heard of for many years would be a far more independent stroke, and it would leave her entirely unfettered. Perhaps he might rival in this kind the accomplished Mr Bellston, of whose journeyings he had heard so much.

He sat and sat, and the fog rose out of the river, enveloping him like a fleece; first his feet and knees, then his arms and body, and finally submerging his head. When he had come to a decision he went up again into the homestead. He would be independent, if he died for it, and he would free Christine. Exile was the only course. The first step was to inform his uncle of his determination.

Two days later Nicholas was on the same spot in the mead, at almost the same hour of eve. But there was no fog now; a blusterous autumn wind had ousted the still, golden days and misty nights; and he was going, full of purpose, in the opposite direction. When he had last entered the mead he was an inhabitant of the Swenn valley; in forty-eight hours he had severed himself from that spot as completely as if he had never belonged to it. All that appertained to him in the Swenn valley now was circumscribed by the portmanteau in his hand.

In making his preparations for departure he had unconsciously held a faint, foolish hope that she would communicate with him and make up their estrangement in some soft womanly way. But she had given no signal, and it was too evident to him that her latest mood had grown to be her fixed one, proving how well-founded had been his impulse to set her free.

He entered the Sallows, found his way in the dark to the garden-door of the house, slipped under it a note to tell her of his departure, and explaining its true reason to be a consciousness of her growing feeling that he was an encumbrance and a humiliation. Of the direction of his journey and of the date of his return he said nothing.

His course now took him into the high road, which he pursued for some miles in a north-easterly direction, still spinning the thread of sad inferences, and asking himself why he should ever return. At daybreak he stood on the hill above Shottsford-Forum, and awaited a coach which passed about this time along that highway towards Salisbury and London.

VI

Some fifteen years after the date of the foregoing incidents, a man who had dwelt in far countries, and viewed many cities, arrived at Troyton Inn, an isolated tavern on the old western turnpike-road, not five miles from Swenn-Everard. He was still barely of middle-age, but it could be seen that a haze of grey was settling upon the locks of his hair, and that his face had lost colour and curve, as if by exposure to bleaching climates and strange atmospheres, or from ailments contracted therein. He seemed to observe little around him, by reason of the intrusion of his musings upon the scene. In truth Nicholas Long was just now the creature of old hopes and fears consequent upon his arrival—this man who once had not cared if his name were blotted out from that district. The evening light showed wistful lines which he could not smooth out by the worldling's gloss of nonchalance that he had learnt to fling over his face.

Troyton Inn was a somewhat unusual place for a man of this sort to choose as a house of sojourn. Before he left home it had been a lively old tavern at which High-flyers, and Heralds, and Tally-hoes had changed horses on their stages up and down the country; but now the house was rather cavernous and chilly, the stable-roofs were hollow-backed, the landlord was asthmatic, and the traffic gone.

He arrived in the afternoon, and when he had sent back the fly and was having a nondescript meal, he put a question to the waiting-maid, with a mien of indifference.

'Squire Everard, of Swenn-Everard Manor, has been dead some years, I believe?'

She replied in the affirmative.

'And are any of the family left there still?'

'Oh no, bless you, sir! They sold the place years ago—Squire Everard's son did—and went away. I've never heard where they went to. They came quite to nothing.'

'Never heard anything of the young lady—the Squire's daughter?'

'No. You see 'twas before I came to these parts.'

When the waitress had left the room, Nicholas pushed

aside his plate and gazed out of the window. He was not going over into the Swenn Valley altogether on Christine's account, but she had greatly animated his motive in coming that way. Anyhow he would push on there now that he was so near, and not ask questions here where he was liable to be wrongly informed. The fundamental inquiry he had not ventured to make—whether Christine had married before the family went away. He had abstained because of an absurd dread of extinguishing hopeful surmise. That the Everards had left their old home was bad enough intelligence for one day.

Rising from the table he put on his hat and went out, ascending towards the upland which divided this district from his native vale. The first familiar feature that met his eye was a little spot on the distant sky—a clump of trees standing on a barrow which surmounted a yet more remote upland—a point where, in his childhood, he had believed people could stand and see America. He reached the further verge of the plateau on which he had entered. Ah, there was the valley—a greenish-grey stretch of colour—still looking placid and serene, as though it had not much missed him. If Christine was no longer there, why should he pause over it this evening? His uncle and aunt were dead, and tomorrow would be soon enough to inquire for remoter relatives. Thus, disinclined to go further, he turned to retrace his way to the inn.

In the backward path he now perceived the figure of a woman, who had been walking at a distance behind him; and as she drew nearer he began to be startled. Surely, despite the variations introduced into that figure by changing years, its ground-lines were those of Christine?

Nicholas had been sentimental enough to write to Christine immediately on landing at Southampton a day or two before this, addressing his letter at a venture to the old house, and merely telling her that he planned to reach Troyton Inn on the present afternoon. The news of the scattering of the Everards had dissipated his hope of hearing of her; but here she was.

So they met—there, alone, on the open down by a pond, just as if the meeting had been carefully arranged.

She threw up her veil. She was still beautiful, though the years had touched her; a little more matronly—much more homely. Or was it only that he was much less homely now— a man of the world—the sense of homeliness being relative? Her face had grown to be pre-eminently of the sort that would be called interesting. Her habiliments were of a demure and sober cast, though she was one who had used to dress so airily and so gaily. Years had laid on a few shadows too in this.

'I received your letter,' she said, when the momentary embarrassment of their first approach had passed. 'And I thought I would walk across the hills today, as it was fine. I have just called at the inn, and they told me you were out. I was now on my way homeward.'

He hardly listened to this, though he intently gazed at her. 'Christine,' he said; 'one word. Are you free?'

'I—I am in a certain sense,' she replied, colouring.

The announcement had a magical effect. The intervening time between past and present closed up for him, and moved by impulse which he had combated for fifteen years, he seized her two hands and drew her towards him.

She started back, and became almost a mere acquaintance. 'I have to tell you,' she gasped, 'that I have—been married.'

Nicholas's rose-coloured dream was immediately toned down to a greyish tinge.

'I did not marry till many years after you left,' she continued in the humble tones of one confessing to a crime. 'Oh Nic,' she cried reproachfully, 'how could you stay away so long!'

'Whom did you marry?'

'Mr Bellston.'

'I—ought to have expected it.' He was going to add, 'And is he dead?' but he checked himself. Her dress unmistakably suggested widowhood; and she had said she was free.

'I must now hasten home,' said she. 'I felt that, considering my shortcomings at our parting so many years ago, I owed you the initiative now.'

'There is some of your old generosity in that. I'll walk with you, if I may. Where are you living, Christine?'

'In the same house, but not on the old conditions. I have part of it on lease; the farmer now tenanting the premises found the whole more than he wanted, and the owner allowed me to keep what rooms I chose. I am poor now, you know, Nicholas, and almost friendless. My brother sold the Swenn-Everard estate when it came to him, and the person who bought it turned our home into a farm-house. Till my father's death my husband and I lived in the manor-house with him, so that I have never lived away from the spot.'

She was poor. That, and the change of name, sufficiently accounted for the inn-servant's ignorance of her continued existence within the walls of her old home.

It was growing dusk, and he still walked with her. A woman's head arose from the declivity before them, and as she drew nearer, Christine asked him to go back. 'This is the wife of the farmer who shares the house,' she said. 'She is accustomed to come out and meet me whenever I walk far and am benighted. I am obliged to walk everywhere now.'

The farmer's wife, seeing that Christine was not alone, paused in her advance, and Nicholas said, 'Dear Christine, if you are obliged to do these things, I am not, and what wealth I can command you may command likewise. They say rolling stones gather no moss; but they gather dross sometimes. I was one of the pioneers to the gold-fields, you know, and made a sufficient fortune there for my wants. What is more, I kept it. When I had done this I was coming home, but hearing of my uncle's death I changed my plan, travelled, speculated, and increased my fortune. Now, before we part: you remember you stood with me at the altar once, and therefore I speak with less preparation than I should otherwise use. Before we part then I ask, shall another again intrude between us? Or shall we complete the union we began?'

She trembled—just as she had done at that very minute of standing with him in the church, to which he had recalled her mind. 'I will not enter into that now, dear Nicholas,' she replied. 'There will be more to talk of and consider first—more to explain, which it would have spoiled this meeting to have entered into now.'

'Yes, yes; but—'

'Further than the brief answer I first gave, Nic, don't press me tonight. I still have the old affection for you, or I should not have sought you. Let that suffice for the moment.'

'Very well, dear one. And when shall I call to see you?'

'I will write and fix an hour. I will tell you everything of my history then.'

And thus they parted, Nicholas feeling that he had not come here fruitlessly. When she and her companion were out of sight he retraced his steps to Troyton, where he made himself as comfortable as he could in the deserted old inn of his boyhood's days. He missed her companionship this evening more than he had done at any time during the whole fifteen years; and it was as though instead of separation there had been constant communion with her throughout that period. The tones of her voice had stirred his heart in places which had lain stagnant ever since he last heard them. They recalled the woman to whom he had once lifted his eyes as to a goddess. Her announcement that she had been another's came as a little shock to him, and he did not now lift his eyes to her in precisely the same way as he had lifted them at first. But he forgave her for marrying Bellston; what could he expect after fifteen years?

He slept at Troyton Inn that night, and in the morning there was a short note from her, repeating more emphatically her statement of the previous evening—that she wished to inform him clearly of her circumstances, and to calmly consider with him the position in which she was placed. Would he call upon her on Sunday afternoon, when she was sure to be alone?

'Nic,' she wrote on, 'what a cosmopolite you are! I expected to find my old yeoman still; but I was quite awed in the presence of such a citizen of the world. Did I seem rusty and unpractised? Ah—you seemed so once to me!'

Tender, playful words; the old Christine was in them. She said Sunday afternoon, and it was now only Saturday morning. He wished she had said today; that short revival of her image had vitalized to sudden heat feelings that had almost been stilled. Whatever she might have to explain as to her position—and it was awkwardly narrowed, no doubt—he could not give her up. Miss Everard or Mrs Bellston, what mattered it?—she was the same Christine.

He did not go outside the inn all Saturday. He had no wish to see or do anything but to await the coming interview. So he smoked, and read the local newspaper of the previous week, and stowed himself in the chimney-corner. In the evening he felt that he could remain indoors no longer, and the moon being near the full, he started from the inn on foot in the same direction as that of yesterday, with the view of contemplating the old village and its precincts, and hovering round her house under the cloak of night.

With a stout stick in his hand he climbed over the five miles of upland in a comparatively short space of time. Nicholas had seen many strange lands and trodden many strange ways since he last walked that path, but as he trudged he seemed wonderfully like his old self, and had not the slightest difficulty in finding the way. In descending to the meads the streams perplexed him a little, some of the old foot-bridges having been removed; but he ultimately got across the larger water-courses, and pushed on to the village, avoiding her residence for the moment, lest she should encounter him, and think he had not respected the time of her appointment.

He found his way to the churchyard, and first ascertained where lay the two relations he had left alive at his departure; then he observed the gravestones of other inhabitants with whom he had been well acquainted, till by degrees he seemed to be in the society of all the elder Swenn-Everard population, as he had known the place. Side by side as they had lived in his day here were they now. They had moved house in mass.

But no tomb of Mr Bellston was visible, though, as he had lived at the manor-house, it would have been natural to find it here. In truth Nicholas was more anxious to discover that than anything, being curious to know how long he had been dead. Seeing from the glimmer of a light in the church that somebody was there cleaning for Sunday he entered, and looked round upon the walls as well as he could. But there was no monument to her husband, though one had been erected to the Squire.

Nicholas addressed the young man who was sweeping. 'I don't see any monument or tomb to the late Mr Bellston?'

'Oh no, sir; you won't see that,' said the young man drily.

'Why, pray?'

'Because he's not buried here. He's not Christian-buried anywhere, as far as we know. In short, perhaps he's not buried at all; and between ourselves, perhaps he's alive.'

Nicholas sank an inch shorter. 'Ah,' he answered.

'Then you don't know the peculiar circumstances, sir?'

'I am a stranger here—as to late years.'

'Mr Bellston was a traveller—an explorer—it was his calling; you may have heard his name as such?'

'I remember.' Nicholas recalled the fact that this very bent of Mr Bellston's was the incentive to his own roaming.

'Well, when he married he came and lived here with his wife and his wife's father, and said he would travel no more. But after a time he got weary of biding quiet here, and weary of her— he was not a good husband to the young lady by any means— and he betook himself again to his old trick of roving—with her money. Away he went, quite out of the realm of human foot, into the bowels of Asia, and never was heard of more. He was murdered, it is said, but nobody knows; though as that was nine years ago he's dead enough in principle, if not in corporation. His widow lives quite humble, for between her husband and her brother she's left in very lean pasturage.'

Nicholas went back to Troyton Inn without hovering round her dwelling. This then was the explanation which she had wanted to make. Not dead, but missing. How could he have expected that the first fair promise of happiness held out to him would remain untarnished? She had said that she was free; and legally she was free, no doubt. Moreover, from her tone and manner he felt himself justified in concluding that she would be willing to run the risk of a union with him, in the improbability of her husband's existence. Even if that husband lived, his return was not a likely event, to judge from his character. A man who could spend her money on his own personal adventures would not be anxious to disturb her poverty after such a lapse of time.

Well, the prospect was not so unclouded as it had seemed. But could he, even now, give up Christine?

VII

Two months more brought the year nearly to a close, and found Nicholas Long tenant of a spacious house in the market-town nearest to Swenn-Everard. A man of means, genial character, and a bachelor, he was an object of great interest to his neighbours, and to his neighbours' wives and daughters. But he took little note of this, and had made it his business to go twice a-week, no matter what the weather, to the now farm-house at Swenn-Everard, a wing of which had been retained as the refuge of Christine. He always walked, to give no trouble in putting up a horse to a housekeeper whose staff was limited.

The two had put their heads together on the situation, had gone to a solicitor, had balanced possibilities, and had resolved to make the plunge of matrimony. 'Nothing venture nothing have,' Christine had said, with some of her old audacity.

With almost gratuitous honesty they had let their intentions be widely known. Christine, it is true, had rather shrunk from publicity at first; but Nicholas argued that their boldness in this respect would have good results. With his friends he held that there was not the slightest probability of her being other than a widow, and a challenge to the missing man now, followed by no response, would stultify any unpleasant remarks which might be thrown at her after their union. To this end a paragraph was inserted in the Wessex papers, announcing that their marriage was proposed to be celebrated on such and such a day in December.

His periodic walks along the south side of the valley to visit her were among the happiest experiences of his life. The yellow leaves falling around him in the foreground, the well-watered meads on the right hand, and the woman he loved awaiting him at the back of the scene, promised a future of much serenity, as far as human judgment could foresee. On arriving, he would sit with her in the 'parlour' of the wing she retained, her general sitting-room, where the only relics of her early surroundings were an old clock from the other end of the house, and her own piano. Before it was quite dark they would stand, hand in hand, looking out of the window across the flat turf to the dark clump of trees which hid further view from their eyes.

'Do you wish you were still mistress here, dear?' he once said.

'Not at all,' said she cheerfully. 'I have a good enough room, and a good enough fire, and a good enough friend. Besides, my latter days as mistress of the house were not happy ones, and they spoilt the place for me. It was a punishment for my faithfulness. Nic, you do forgive me? Really you do?'

The twenty-third of December, the eve of the wedding-day, had arrived at last in the train of such uneventful ones as these. Nicholas had arranged to visit her that day a little later than usual, and see that everything was ready with her for the morrow's event and her removal to his house; for he had begun to look after her domestic affairs, and to lighten as much as possible the duties of her housekeeping.

He was to come to an early supper, which she had arranged to take the place of a wedding-breakfast next day— the latter not being feasible in her present situation. An hour or so after dark the wife of the farmer who lived in the other part of the house entered Christine's parlour to lay the cloth.

'What with getting the ham skinned, and the black-puddings hotted up,' she said; 'it will take me all my time before he's here, if I begin this minute.'

'I'll lay the table myself,' said Christine, jumping up. 'Do you attend to the cooking.'

'Thank you, ma'am. And perhaps 'tis no matter, seeing that it is the last night you'll have to do such work. I knew this sort of life wouldn't last long for ye, being born to better things.'

'It has lasted rather long, Mrs Wake. And if he had not found me out it would have lasted all my days.'

'But he did find you out.'

'He did. And I'll lay the cloth immediately.'

Mrs Wake went back to the kitchen, and Christine began to bustle about. She greatly enjoyed preparing this table for Nicholas and herself with her own hands. She took artistic pleasure in adjusting each article to its position, as if half an inch error were a point of high importance. Finally she placed the two candles where they were to stand, and sat down by the fire.

Mrs Wake re-entered and regarded the effect. 'Why not have another candle or two, ma'am?' she said. ''Twould make it livelier. Say four.'

'Very well,' said Christine; and four candles were lighted. 'Really,' she added, surveying them, 'I have been now so long accustomed to little economies that they look quite extravagant.'

'Ah, you'll soon think nothing of forty in his grand new house! Shall I bring in supper directly he comes, ma'am?'

'No, not for half an hour; and, Mrs Wake, you and Betsy are busy in the kitchen, I know; so when he knocks don't disturb yourselves; I can let him in.'

She was again left alone, and, as it still wanted some time to Nicholas's appointment, she stood by the fire, looking at herself in the glass over the mantel. Reflectively raising a lock of her hair just above her temple she uncovered a small scar. That scar had a history. The terrible temper of her late husband—those sudden moods of irascibility which had made even his friendly excitements look like anger—had once caused him to set that mark upon her with the bezel of a ring he wore. He declared that the whole thing was an accident. She was a woman, and kept her own opinion.

Christine then turned her back to the glass and scanned

the table and the candles, shining one at each corner like types of the four Evangelists, and thought they looked too assuming—too confident. She glanced up at the clock, which stood also in this room, there not being space enough for it in the passage. It was nearly seven, and she expected Nicholas at half-past. She liked the company of this venerable article in her lonely life: its tickings and whizzings were a sort of conversation. It now began to strike the hour. At the end something grated slightly. Then without any warning, the clock slowly inclined forward and fell at full length upon the floor.

The crash brought the farmer's wife rushing into the room. Christine had well-nigh sprung out of her shoes. Mrs Wake's inquiry what had happened was answered by the evidence of her own eyes.

'How did it occur?' she said.

'I cannot say; it was not firmly fixed, I suppose. Dear me, how sorry I am! My dear father's hall-clock! And now I suppose it is ruined.'

Assisted by Mrs Wake, she lifted the clock. Every inch of glass was, of course, shattered, but very little harm besides appeared to be done. They propped it up temporarily, though it would not go again.

Christine had soon recovered her composure, but she saw that Mrs Wake was gloomy. 'What does it mean, Mrs Wake?' she said. 'Is it ominous?'

'It is a sign of a violent death in the family.'

'Don't talk of it. I don't believe such things; and don't mention it to Mr Long when he comes. *He's* not in the family yet, you know.'

'Oh, no, it cannot refer to him,' said Mrs Wake musingly.

'Some remote cousin, perhaps,' observed Christine, no less willing to humour her than to get rid of a shapeless dread which the incident had caused in her own mind. 'And— supper is almost ready, Mrs Wake?'

'In three-quarters of an hour.'

Mrs Wake left the room, and Christine sat on. Though it still wanted fifteen minutes to the hour at which Nicholas had promised to be there, she began to grow impatient. After the accustomed ticking the dead silence was oppressive. But she had not to wait so long as she had expected; steps were heard approaching the door, and there was a knock.

Christine was already there to open to it. The entrance had no lamp, but it was not particularly dark out of doors. She could see the outline of a man, and cried cheerfully, 'You are early; it is very good of you.'

'Early am I? I thought I was late.'

The voice was not the voice of Nicholas.

'I beg pardon,' said she. 'I did not—I expected some one else. Will you come in? You wish to see Mrs Wake?'

The new-comer did not answer, but followed her up the passage and into her own room. She turned to look at him, and by degrees recognized that her husband, James Bellston, stood before her.

She sank into a chair. He was now a much-bearded man, his beard growing almost straight from his face like spines. Corpulent he was too, and short in his breathing, but unmistakable. He placed a small leather portmanteau of a common kind on the floor and said, 'You did not expect me?'

'I did not,' she gasped. 'I thought you were—'

'Dead. Good. So did others. It was natural, Christine, and I have a good deal to blame myself for in that respect; but I could bring you home neither money nor fame, and what was the use of my coming? However, I heard, or rather read, the account of your approaching marriage, and that forced my hand. It was to have been tomorrow?'

'Yes.'

'I knew by seeing the date mentioned in the papers. That was why I came tonight, though I had the greatest difficulty in getting here, owing to my having taken passage in a sailing vessel, which was delayed by contrary winds. I meant to have arrived much sooner. And so the old house and manor are gone from your family at last?' he said, seating himself.

'Yes,' said she; and then she spasmodically began to tell him of things that were more pertinent to the moment—how Nicholas Long had come back a comparatively rich man; that he was going to call that evening, and that the very supper-table before their eyes was laid for him.

'Then he may enter at any minute?' said her husband.

'Certainly.'

'That will be awkward. In common civility he ought to be forewarned. All this comes of my being so delayed . . . My dear, I think the proper plan will be for me to go out for half-an-hour, during which time he will arrive, I presume. You can break to him what has happened, and please convey my apologies to him for this abrupt return, which I really could not help. I will come back to the house when he is gone, and so an unpleasant encounter will be avoided. If I allow him an hour from this time to be out of the house it will be long enough probably?'

'Yes. And the supper—'

'Can wait till I come. Thank you, dear. Now I'll go and stroll round, and see how the familiar old places look after such a long interval.'

He placed his portmanteau in a corner, imprinted a business-like kiss upon her cheek, and withdrew.

She was alone; but what a solitude!

She stood in the middle of the room just as he had left her, in the gloomy silence of the stopped clock, till at length she heard another tread without, coming from an opposite direction to that of her husband's retreat, and there was a second knocking at the door.

She did not respond to it; and Nicholas—for it was he—thinking that he was not heard by reason of concentration on tomorrow's proceedings, opened the door softly, and came on to the door of her room, which stood unclosed, just as it had been left by her husband.

Nicholas uttered a blithe greeting, cast his eye round the parlour, which with its tall candles, blazing fire, snow-white cloth, and prettily-spread table, formed a cheerful spectacle enough for a man who had been walking in the dark for an hour.

'My bride—almost, at last!' he cried, encircling her with his arms.

Instead of responding, her figure became limp, frigid, heavy; her head fell back, and he found that she had fainted.

It was natural, he thought. She had had many little worrying matters to attend to, and but slight assistance. He ought to have seen more effectually to her affairs; the closeness of the event had over-excited her. Nicholas kissed her unconscious face—more than once, little thinking whose lips had lately made a lodging there. Loth to call Mrs Wake, he carried Christine to a couch and laid her down. This had the effect of reviving her. Nicholas bent and whispered in her ear, 'Lie quiet, dearest, no hurry; and dream, dream, dream of happy days. It is only I. You will soon be better.' He held her by the hand.

'No, no, no!' she moaned. 'Oh, how can this be?'

Nicholas was alarmed and perplexed, but the disclosure was not long delayed. When she had sat up, and by degrees made the stunning event known to him, he stood as if transfixed.

'Ah—is it so!' said he. Then, becoming quite meek, 'And why was he so cruel as to—delay his return till now?'

She dutifully recited the explanation her husband had given her; but her mechanical manner of telling it showed how much she doubted its truth. It was too unlikely that his arrival at such a dramatic moment should not be a contrived surprise, quite of a piece with his previous dealings towards her.

'He—seems very kind now—not as he used to be,' she faltered. 'And perhaps, Nicholas, he is a changed man—we'll hope he is. I suppose I ought not to have listened to my legal advisers, and assumed his death so surely! Anyhow, I am roughly received back into—the right way!'

Nicholas burst out bitterly: 'Oh what too, too honest fools we were!—to so court daylight upon our intention! Why could we not have married privately, and gone away, so that he would never have known what had become of you, even if he had returned? Christine, he has done it to . . . But I'll say no more. Of course we—might fly now.'

'No, no; we might not,' said she hastily.

'Very well. But this is hard to bear! "When I looked for good then evil came unto me, and when I waited for light there came darkness." So once said a sorely tried man in the land of Uz, and so say I now! . . . Is he near at this moment?'

She told him how Bellston had gone out for a short walk whilst she broke the news; that he would be in soon.

'And is this meal laid for him, or for me?'

'It was laid for you.'

'And it will be eaten by him?'

'Yes.'

'Christine, are you *sure* that he is come, or have you been sleeping over the fire and dreaming it?'

She pointed to the portmanteau in the corner, with the initials 'J.B.' in white letters.

'Well, goodbye—goodbye! Curse that parson for not marrying us fifteen years ago!'

It is unnecessary to dwell further upon that parting. There are scenes wherein the words spoken do not even approximate to the level of the mental communion between the actors. Suffice it to say that part they did, and quickly; and Nicholas, more dead than alive, went out of the house homewards.

Why had he ever come back? During his absence he had not cared for Christine as he cared now. His last state was worse than his first. He was more than once tempted to descend into the meads instead of keeping along their edge. The Swenn was down there, and he knew of quiet pools in that stream to which death would come easily. One thought, however, kept him from seriously contemplating any desperate act. His affection for her was strongly protective, and in the event of her requiring a friend's support in future troubles there was none but himself left in the world to afford it. So he walked on.

Meanwhile Christine had resigned herself to circumstances. A resolve to continue worthy of her history and of her family lent her heroism and dignity. She called Mrs Wake, and explained to that worthy woman as much of what had occurred as she deemed necessary. Mrs Wake was too amazed to reply; she retreated slowly, her lips parted; till at the door she said with a dry mouth, 'And the beautiful supper, ma'am?'

'Serve it when he comes.'

'When Mr Bellston—yes, ma'am, I will.' She still stood gazing, as if she could hardly take in the order.

'That will do, Mrs Wake. I am much obliged to you for all your kindness.' And Christine was left alone again, and then she wept.

She sat down and waited. That awful silence of the stopped clock began anew, but she did not mind it now. She was listening for a footfall, in a state of mental tensity which almost took away from her the power of motion. It seemed to her that the prescribed hour of her husband's absence must have expired; but she was not sure, and waited on.

Mrs Wake again came in. 'You have not rung for supper—'

'He is not yet come, Mrs Wake. If you want to go to bed, bring in the supper and set it on the table. It will be equally good cold. Leave the door unbarred.'

Mrs Wake did as was suggested, made up the fire, and went away. Shortly afterwards Christine heard her retire to her chamber. But Christine still sat on, and still her husband postponed his entry.

She aroused herself once or twice to make up the fire, but was ignorant how the night was going. Her watch was upstairs and she did not make the effort to go up to consult it. In her seat she continued; and still the supper waited, and still he did not come.

At length she was so nearly persuaded that his visit must have been a dream after all, that she again went over to his portmanteau, felt it and examined it. His it unquestionably was; it was unlocked, and contained only some common articles of wearing apparel. She sighed and sat down again.

Presently she fell into a doze, and when she again became conscious she found that the four candles had burnt into their sockets and gone out. The fire still emitted a feeble shine. Christine did not take the trouble to get more candles, but stirred the fire and sat on.

After a long period she heard a creaking of the chamber floor and stairs at the other end of the house, and knew that the farmer's family were getting up. By-and-by Mrs Wake entered the room, candle in hand, bouncing open the door in her morning manner, obviously without any expectation of finding a person there.

'Lord-a-mercy! What sitting here again, ma'am?'

'Yes, I am sitting here still.'

'You've been there ever since last night?'

'Yes.'

'Then—'

'He's not come.'

'Well, he won't come at this time o' morning,' said the farmer's wife. 'Do 'ee get on to bed, ma'am. You must be scrammed to death!'

It occurred to Christine now that possibly her husband had thought better of obtruding himself upon her company within an hour of revealing his existence to her, and had decided to pay a more formal visit next day. She therefore adopted Mrs Wake's suggestion and retired.

VIII

Nicholas had gone straight home, neither speaking to nor seeing a soul. From that hour a change seemed to come over him. He had ever possessed a full share of self-consciousness; he had been readily piqued, had shown an unusual dread of being personally obtrusive. But now his sense of self, as an individual provoking opinion, appeared to leave him. When, therefore, after a day or two of seclusion, he came forth again, and the few acquaintances he had formed in the town condoled with him on what had happened, and pitied his haggard looks, he did not shrink from their regard as he would have done formerly, but took their sympathy as it would have been accepted by a child.

It reached his ears that Bellston had not reappeared on the evening of his arrival, either at his wife's house or at any hotel in the town or neighbourhood. 'That's a part of his cruelty,' thought Nicholas. And when two or three days had passed, and still no account came to him of Bellston having joined her, he ventured to set out for Swenn-Everard.

Christine was so shaken that she was obliged to receive him as she lay on a sofa, beside the square table which was to have borne their evening feast. She fixed her eyes wistfully upon him, and smiled a sad smile.

'He has not come back?' said Nicholas under his breath.

'He has not.'

Then Nicholas sat beside her, and they talked on general topics merely like saddened old friends. But they could not keep away the subject of Bellston, their voices dropping as it forced its way in. Christine, no less than Nicholas, knowing her husband's character, inferred that, having stopped her game, as he would have phrased it, he was taking things leisurely, and, finding nothing very attractive in her limited mode of living, was meaning to return to her only when he had nothing better to do.

The bolt which laid low their hopes had struck so recently, that they could hardly look each other in the face when speaking that day. But when a week or two had passed, and all the horizon still remained as vacant of Bellston as before, Nicholas and she could talk of the event with calm wonderment. Why had he come, to go again like this?

And then there set in a period of resigned surmise, during which

'So like, so very like, was day to day,'

that to tell of one of them is to tell of all. Nicholas would arrive between three and four in the afternoon, a faint trepidation influencing his walk as he neared her door. He would knock; she would always reply in person, having watched for him from the window. Then he would whisper—

'He has not come back?'

'He has not,' she would say.

Nicholas would enter then, and she being ready bonneted, they would walk into the Sallows together as far as the waterfall, the spot which they had frequently made their place of appointment in their youthful days. A plank bridge, which Bellston had caused to be thrown over the fall during his residence with her in the manor-house, was now again removed, and all was just the same as in Nicholas's time, when he had been accustomed to wade across on the edge of the cascade and come up to her like a merman from the deep. Here on the felled trunk, which still lay rotting in its old place, they would now sit, gazing at the descending sheet of water, with its neverending sarcastic hiss at their baffled attempts to make themselves one flesh. Returning to the house they would sit down together to tea, after which, and the confidential chat that accompanied it, he walked home by the declining light. This proceeding became as periodic as an astronomical recurrence.

Twice a week he came—all through that winter, all through the spring following, through the summer, through the autumn, the next winter, the next year, and the next, till an appreciable span of human life had passed by. Bellston still tarried.

Years and years Nic walked that way, at this interval of three days, from his house in the neighbouring town; and in every instance the aforesaid order of things was customary; and still on his arrival the form of words went on—

'He has not come back?'

'He has not.'

So they grew older. The dim shape of that third one stood continually between them; they could not displace it; neither, on the other hand, could it effectually part them. They were in close communion, yet not indissolubly united; lovers, yet never cured of love. By the time that the fifth year of his visiting had arrived, on about the five-hundredth occasion of his presence at her tea-table, he noticed that the bleaching process which had begun upon his own locks was also spreading to hers. He told her so, and they laughed. Yet she was in good health: a condition of suspense, which would have half-killed a man, had been endured by her without complaint, and even with composure.

One day, when these years of abeyance had numbered seven, they had strolled as usual as far as the waterfall, whose faint roar formed a sort of calling voice sufficient in the circumstances to direct their listlessness. Pausing there, he looked up at her face and said, 'Why should we not try again, Christine? We are legally at liberty to do so now. Nothing venture nothing have.'

But she would not. Perhaps a little primness of idea was by this time ousting the native daring of Christine. 'What he has done once he can do twice,' she said. 'He is not dead, and if we were to marry he would say we had "forced his hand", as he said before, and duly reappear.'

Some years after, when Christine was about fifty, and Nicholas fifty-three, a new trouble of a minor kind arrived. He found an inconvenience in traversing the distance between their two houses, particularly in damp weather, the years he had spent in trying climates abroad having sown the seeds of rheumatism, which made a journey undesirable on inclement days, even in a carriage. He told her of this new difficulty, as he did of everything.

'If you could live nearer,' suggested she.

Unluckily there was no house near. But Nicholas, though not a millionaire, was a man of means; he obtained a small piece of ground on lease at the nearest spot to her home that it could be so obtained, which was on the opposite brink of the Swenn, this river forming the boundary of the Swenn-Everard manor; and here he built a house large enough for his wants. This took time, and when he got into it he found its situation a great comfort to him. He was not more than two hundred yards from her now, and gained a new pleasure in feeling that all sounds which greeted his ears, in the day or in the night, also fell upon hers—the caw of a particular rook, the voice of a neighbouring nightingale, the whistle of a local breeze, or the purl of the fall in the meadows, whose rush was a material rendering of Time's ceaseless scour over themselves, wearing them away without uniting them.

Christine's missing husband was taking shape as a myth among the surrounding residents; but he was still believed in as corporeally imminent by Christine herself, and also, in a milder degree, by Nicholas. For a curious unconsciousness of the long lapse of time since his revelation of himself seemed to affect the pair. There had been no passing events to serve as chronological milestones, and the evening on which she had kept supper waiting for him still loomed out with startling nearness in their retrospects.

In the seventeenth pensive year of this their parallel march towards the common bourne, a labourer came in a hurry one day to Nicholas's house and brought strange tidings. The present owner of Swenn-Everard—a non-resident—had been improving his property in sundry ways, and one of these was by dredging the stream which, in the course of years, had become choked with mud and weeds in its passage through the Sallows. The process necessitated a reconstruction of the waterfall. When the river had been pumped dry for this purpose, the skeleton of a man had been found jammed among the piles supporting the edge of the fall.

Every particle of his flesh and clothing had been eaten by fishes or abraded to nothing by the water, but the relics of a gold watch remained, and on the inside of the case was engraved 'J. Bellston:1838.'

Nicholas, deeply agitated, hastened down to the place and examined the remains attentively, afterwards going across to Christine, and breaking the discovery to her. She would not come to view the skeleton, which lay extended on the grass, not a finger or toe-bone missing, so neatly had the aquatic operators done their work. Conjecture was directed to the question how Bellston had got there; and conjecture alone could give an explanation.

It was supposed that, after calling upon her, he had gone rambling about the grounds, with which he was naturally very familiar, and coming to the fall under the trees had expected to find there the plank by which, during his occupancy of the premises, he had been accustomed to cross into the meads on the other side. Before discovering its removal he had probably overbalanced himself, and was thus precipitated into the cascade, the piles beneath the descending current holding him between them like the prongs of a pitchfork, and effectually preventing the rising of his body, over which the weeds grew. Such was the reasonable supposition concerning the discovery; but proof was never forthcoming.

'To think,' said Nicholas, when the remains had been decently interred, and he was again sitting with Christine—

though not beside the waterfall—'to think how we visited him! How we sat over him, hours and hours, gazing at him, bewailing our fate, when all the time he was ironically hissing at us from the spot, in an unknown tongue, that we could marry if we chose!'

She echoed the sentiment with a sigh.

'You might have married me on the day we had fixed, and there would have been no impediment. You would now have been seventeen years my wife, and we might have had tall sons and daughters.'

'It might have been so,' she murmured.

'Well—is it still better late than never?'

The question was one which had become complicated by the increasing years of each. Their wills were somewhat enfeebled now, their hearts sickened of tender enterprise by hope too long deferred. Having postponed the consideration of their course till a year after the interment of Bellston, each seemed less disposed than formerly to take it up again.

'Is it worth while, after so many years?' she said to him. 'We are fairly happy as we are—perhaps happier than we should be in any other relation, seeing what old people we have grown. The weight is gone from our lives; the shadow no longer divides us: then let us be joyful together as we are, dearest Nic, in the days of our vanity; and

"With mirth and laughter let old wrinkles come!"

• • •

He fell in with these views of hers to some extent. But occasionally he ventured to urge her to reconsider the case, though he spoke not with the fervour of his earlier years.

ACKNOWLEDGMENTS

We gratefully acknowledge all those who gave permission for written material to appear in this book. We have made every effort to trace and contact copyright holders. If an error or omission is brought to our notice we will be pleased to correct the situation in future editions of this book. For further information, please contact the publisher.

Excerpt from *On Love* by Alain de Botton. Copyright © 1993 by Alain de Botton. Used by permission of Grove/Atlantic, Inc. ✤ Excerpt from *Moonlight Shadow* by Banana Yoshimoto. Copyright © 1993 by Banana Yoshimoto. Used by permission of Grove/Atlantic, Inc. ✤ "A Letter That Never Reached Russia" from *The Stories of Vladimir Nabokov* by Vladimir Nabokov, edit., Dmitri Nabokov. Copyright © 1995 by Dmitri Nabokov. Reprinted by permission of Alfred A. Knopf, a Division of Random House, Inc. ✤ "Dulse" from *Selected Stories* by Alice Munro. Copyright © 1996 by Alice Munro. Reprinted by permission of Alfred A. Knopf, a Division of Random House, Inc. ✤ Excerpt from *Hôtel du Lac* by Anita Brookner. Copyright © 1984 by Anita Brookner. Reprinted by permission of Pantheon Books, a division of Random House,

Inc. ✤ "The Bridal Party" by F. Scott Fitzgerald. Copyright ©
1930 by the Curtis Publishing Company. Copyright renewed
© 1958 by Frances Scott Fitzgerald Lanahan. Reprinted with
the permission of Scribner, a Division of Simon & Schuster. ✤
Excerpt from *Sentimental Education* by Gustave Flaubert,
translated by Robert Baldick. Copyright © 1964 by Robert
Baldick. Reprinted by permission of Penguin Books Ltd. UK.
✤ Excerpt from *Swann's Way* by Marcel Proust. Copyright ©
1981 by Random House, Inc. and Chatto & Windus.
Reprinted by permission of Random House, Inc. ✤ "Mid-
Autumn" from *A Good Scent From a Strange Mountain: Stories
by Robert Olen Butler* by Robert Olen Butler. Copyright ©
1992 by Robert Olen Butler. Reprinted by permission of
Henry Holt & Company, LLC. ✤ Excerpt from *The Accidental
Tourist* by Anne Tyler. Copyright © 1985 by Anne Tyler
Modarressi. Reprinted by permission of Alfred A. Knopf, a
Division of Random House, Inc. ✤ Excerpt from *The
Vagabond* by Colette, translated by Enid McLeod. Translation
copyright © 1954, renewed 1982 by FSG, Inc. Reprinted by
permission of Farrar, Straus & Giroux, LLC.

BIBLIOGRAPHY

Brookner, Anita. *Hôtel du Lac*. New York: Vintage Books, 1995.

Butler, Robert Olen. *A Good Scent from a Strange Mountain*. New York: Henry Holt & Company, 1992.

Colette. *The Vagabond*. London: Penguin Books UK, 1960.

De Botton, Alain. *On Love*. New York: Grove Press, 1993.

Fitzgerald, F. Scott. *The Short Stories of F. Scott Fitzgerald*. New York: Simon & Schuster,

Flaubert, Gustave. *Sentimental Education*. London: Penguin Books UK, 1964.

Hardy, Thomas. *The Withered Arm and Other Stories*. London: Penguin Books UK, 1999.

Munro, Alice. *Selected Stories*. New York: Vintage Books, 1997.

Nabokov, Vladimir. *The Stories of Vladimir Nabokov*. New York: Vintage Books, 1997.

Proust, Marcel. *Swann's Way*. New York: Random House, 1981.

Tyler, Anne. *The Accidental Tourist*. New York: Borzoi Books, 1985.

Yoshimoto, Banana. *Kitchen*. New York: Grove Press, 1993.